Puppies in Trouble

Puppy in a Puddle

Illustrations by Ann Baum

Puppies in the Pantry

Illustrations by Shelagh McNicholas

LUCY DANIELS

Hodder
Children's
Books

A division of Hachette Children's Books

This bind-up edition published in 2010
by Hodder Children's Books

Special thanks to Ingrid Hoare
Thanks also to C.J. Hall, B.Vet.Med., M.R.C.V.S., for reviewing
the veterinary information contained in this book.

Animal Ark is a trademark of Working Partners Limited
Text copyright © 1999 Working Partners Limited
Created by Working Partners Limited, London WC1X 9HH
Original series created by Ben M. Baglio
Illustrations copyright © 1999 Ann Baum

Puppy in a Puddle first published as a single volume in Great Britain in 1999
by Hodder Children's Books

The right of Lucy Daniels to be identified as the Author of
the Work has been asserted by her in accordance with the
Copyright, Designs and Patents Act 1988.

1

A Catalogue record for this book is available from the British Library

ISBN 978 1 444 90270 9

Typeset in Baskerville by Avon DataSet Ltd,
Bidford-on-Avon, Warwickshire

The paper and Children's Books
are natural rec in sustainable forests.
The manuf conform to the environmental regulations
of the country of origin.

Puppy
in a
Puddle

To my best friend Tristan Chapman and Hugo,
his wonderful, big puppy.

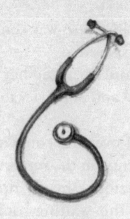

One

'What *is* that smell?' asked Mandy Hope as she walked through the door from her home into the reception at Animal Ark. She wrinkled her nose. 'It smells like a hairdresser's in here!'

Jean Knox, the surgery receptionist, put a finger to her lips. Then, she chuckled. 'It's Toby. I think Mrs Ponsonby has drenched him in her perfume. Apparently he found something rather nasty to roll in – and came home smelling bad enough to cause Pandora to have a fit!'

'Oh no!' Mandy said, grinning. Everyone in Welford knew what a fuss-pot Mrs Ponsonby was where the little Pekinese was concerned. 'Not a real fit?' she whispered.

Jean grinned and shrugged her shoulders. She put on her glasses and went back to the paperwork on her desk.

Mandy looked over the counter to where Mrs Ponsonby was sitting in the surgery waiting-room. Apart from the stout, smartly dressed lady and her two dogs, the waiting-room was empty. The surgery was unusually quiet for a Saturday morning.

Mrs Ponsonby was wafting a lace-edged handkerchief under her nose with one hand and holding her scruffy mongrel pup, Toby, on the lead with the other. Pandora, the Pekinese, sat on Mrs Ponsonby's lap, her long creamy-coloured fur spread out over her owner's flowery dress. The spoilt little dog looked calm and untroubled.

'Hello, Mrs Ponsonby,' Mandy called.

'Mandy, dear!' breathed Mrs Ponsonby, looking up. 'Have you any idea just how much longer your father is likely to be? Only, I rather think this is an emergency visit . . .'

'He's in the middle of an operation, Mrs Ponsonby, but Mrs Hope shouldn't be much longer,' Jean called. 'And there's no one ahead of you in the queue today, so you should be able to go straight in, in a minute or two.'

'Yes,' Mandy said reassuringly. 'It's really quiet for a Saturday morning surgery.'

She slipped out from behind the reception desk and went to say hello to Toby and Pandora. 'What's Pandora's problem, Mrs Ponsonby?' she asked.

'Well,' said Mrs Ponsonby, looking pained, 'Toby arrived in the kitchen this morning reeking of something foul, which upset poor Pandora. I'm certain she had a fit of some kind. She was panting, and her eyes were bulging – it was awful. And then I decided to disguise the dreadful smell with some perfume, but I splashed it in Toby's eye and he gave such a terrible yell . . .'

Mandy noticed that one of Toby's eyes was half-closed, but he seemed to be in his usual high spirits. He wagged his tail happily at Mandy. She stroked his head. The scent of lavender, mingling with the more pungent stench that Toby had so happily rolled in, rose into the air. Mandy coughed. 'Never mind, Toby,' she said. 'We'll have you back to normal in no time. Both of you,' she added, smiling at Pandora. 'Sounds like you've had a bad morning, Mrs Ponsonby.'

'I have, dear,' Mrs Ponsonby sighed.

As Mandy was fussing Toby, the door of one of the treatment rooms opened. She turned round and saw her mother washing her hands at the basin. A man holding a cat in a wicker basket was just leaving the treatment room. 'Thanks so much,' he said. 'I'll bring Cassie back in a day or two. Goodbye.'

'Bye,' said Mrs Hope, drying her hands on a small towel. Toby yapped sharply as the cat let out a mournful wail.

Mandy's mother waved at her through the open door of the treatment room, then spotted Mrs Ponsonby, who was struggling to stand up with Pandora in her arms.

'Hello, Mrs Ponsonby,' Mrs Hope called cheerfully, tucking a few strands of her long red hair behind her ear. 'Come along in. Oh . . . both of them today, is it?' She winked at Mandy, then closed the door.

Jean caught Mandy's eye and they laughed. Mandy wandered over to the window. It was a hot July day, and the green hills beyond the village looked inviting in the sunshine. It wouldn't be long until the start of the school summer holidays, she thought happily. There would be lots of opportunities to help out at Animal Ark once school was finished, and hours of exploring the hills around Welford with her best friend James Hunter and his Labrador, Blackie.

'Ah, here comes a patient!' Mandy told Jean, who was busy with some paperwork. Mandy went to open the surgery door for a visitor she hadn't seen before. He was a tall, tanned man dressed in a blue denim shirt and jeans, and carrying a large cardboard box against his chest. He smiled as Mandy stood aside to let him in.

'Mr Taylor,' he told Jean, propping the edge of the box on the counter. 'And this is Rush. He's come for his twelve-week vaccination.'

'Hello,' Jean smiled. 'Would you just fill out this card for me, please, Mr Taylor? Mr Hope is just finishing a small operation. We won't keep you long.'

'May I see Rush?' Mandy asked Mr Taylor, pointing to the box.

'Sure.' Mr Taylor set the box down on the floor

and lifted the flaps. Then he went back to his card.

Mandy bent down to look inside. Two pink-rimmed blue eyes looked up at her from behind a long fringe of fluffy white fur. A small, black, button-like nose twitched with interest. 'Oh!' she exclaimed. 'He's gorgeous!'

'He's an Old English sheepdog puppy,' Mr Taylor told her with pride, handing the completed card to Jean.

'They were used for moving livestock to market,' Mr Taylor told her. 'The dog's hair was clipped along with the sheep and the hair was woven to make blankets. Did you know that?'

'No, I didn't,' Mandy said. 'I can't imagine him herding sheep!' She grinned. 'Hello, Rush.' Captivated, she gently stroked the puppy's downy little head. 'Aren't you a sweetie?' Rush wagged his stump of a tail and the back end of his body wagged with it. He toppled over comically inside the box, then put both paws on the rim in an effort to get out and climb into Mandy's arms.

'Oh no you don't,' said Mr Taylor, easing him back.

'Mr Taylor and . . . Rush,' called the voice of Adam Hope from the doorway of the treatment room. Mandy looked up at her father and smiled.

'Mr Taylor has an Old English sheepdog pup, Dad,' she told him. 'Can I watch while he has his injection, please?'

'If Mr Taylor doesn't mind.' He smiled and turned to speak to the puppy's owner. 'My daughter wants to be a vet, Mr Taylor,' Adam Hope told his client. 'Just like her parents.'

Mr Taylor readily agreed that Mandy could watch, and carried Rush into the treatment room.

The puppy sat in the box, his furry head just showing over the cardboard rim, peering around uneasily. He sniffed. There was an assortment of confusing smells in the room: disinfectant, medicines, the lingering smell of strong perfume – and other animals. Rush whimpered.

'Put him on the table, please,' Mr Hope said. 'Now, let's have a look at you, little fellow.' He lifted Rush gently out of the box. The puppy's feet splayed out on the slippery surface of the scrubbed metal worktop and Mandy instinctively reached out to stroke and comfort the nervous little dog. She watched her father as he examined Rush, applying gentle pressure to the puppy's abdomen, looking into each ear and opening his mouth to check his teeth and gums.

'Rush is due for his twelve-week vaccination, is that right, Mr Taylor?' he asked. Mandy saw that her father was frowning.

'Yes, he's just twelve weeks now,' said Mr Taylor. He did a quick mental calculation. 'Yes, that's right. We bought him when he was eight weeks old.' He nodded with certainty.

Mandy was still playing with the puppy, who now seemed quite at ease. He peeped out over the crook of her sun-tanned elbow and blinked.

'Strange,' murmured Adam Hope, opening Rush's mouth a second time. 'He looks younger than twelve weeks. Of course, he could just be a late developer, but it's unusual.'

'Where did you get him?' Mandy asked, half wishing she could have a puppy herself.

'I bought him from a breeder on the road to Walton,' Mr Taylor replied. 'Mrs Merrick.'

'Ah, yes,' said Mr Hope. 'I know of her, but we haven't met. Katharine Merrick. She has a good reputation.' He frowned as he put his stethoscope on Rush's chest. 'He seems in good shape – but I'm going to hold off giving him that shot today, Mr Taylor. I'm sure that he's still too young for the vaccination.'

'Really? Well, shall I come back in another couple of weeks, then?' Mr Taylor asked, while Mandy stroked the puppy. Rush licked her cheek with a tiny pink tongue.

'Yes, if you don't mind. I'll give you a wormer for him . . .' Mr Hope turned away and rustled about in a cupboard on the far side of the small room. He came back to the table. He was writing out the instructions on the packet of worming medicine when his stethoscope slipped from round his neck. It clattered loudly on to the table behind Rush. Mandy jumped. 'Dad!'

'Sorry, love,' said Mr Hope. He frowned. 'Now, that is odd.'

'Odd?' asked Mr Taylor. 'What's odd?'

'Well,' began Mr Hope, 'Rush didn't react at all to that loud noise just behind him. It was as though he didn't hear a thing . . . Mandy, distract him by playing with him for a minute, will you?'

Mandy leaned forward and blew gently on the puppy's face. Rush sneezed and shook his head, then began to chew on her fingers, making a small growling sound, as if pretending to be fierce.

'That's right,' said her dad softly. 'Now, I'm going to clap my hands behind him and see if he reacts.' There was a sharp crack as Adam Hope's palms came together. The puppy didn't move, or look round. He sat with his head cocked to one side, looking at Mandy.

'Do you think he's deaf?' asked Mr Taylor.

'I'm afraid it looks that way,' Mr Hope said sadly.

'Oh, no . . . That's awful! Poor little thing,' said Mandy, hugging the little puppy, who looked perfectly happy.

'We thought it was strange that he didn't seem to have learned his name,' Mr Taylor said. 'He doesn't come when he's called either, but we assumed that was because he was so young – and just disobedient.'

'I'm sorry,' said Adam Hope, taking another look in Rush's ear. 'The exterior part of both ears seems perfectly healthy. There's no blockage. I suspect this is a problem with the nerves inside the ear, in which case it's likely he was born that way. What we need to do is to check up on his littermates, and on his parents, to see if it runs in the family. I think it would be a good idea if you get hold of Mrs Merrick and explain the problem.'

'Yes, I will. But what can you do for Rush?' asked Mr Taylor, sounding concerned.

'I'm afraid there's nothing I can do to restore his hearing,' Mr Hope explained sympathetically. 'It will be difficult to train him, but he's not going to suffer. He's not in any pain. You'll need to keep him in a secure environment and make sure he's always on a lead when he's out and about. He won't be able to hear the noise of traffic, of course, so you'll need to take extra care on the roads. Do speak to Mrs Merrick, though,' he added. 'Information about the other puppies in the litter will be useful. Did you meet the parent dogs when you bought Rush?' Mr Hope asked.

'Um . . . no,' Mr Taylor said. 'No, come to think of it, there didn't seem to be any adult dogs around.'

'Hmm.' Adam Hope looked thoughtful. 'It's never a good idea to buy a puppy without having seen it with its mother. But there you are. Bring him back to me for that shot in about three weeks' time.'

'I will,' said Mr Taylor, putting Rush back into the box. 'Thanks.'

'Good luck,' said Mr Hope.

'Bye, Rush,' Mandy said in a small voice. She felt sad to think of the puppy growing up in a world of silence.

When morning surgery was over, Mandy found her mother relaxing at the kitchen table, drinking a mug of tea, with the morning papers spread out in front of her.

'Has Dad finished yet, love?' Mrs Hope asked.

'Yep. Not really a busy morning, was it?' Mandy replied as she pulled out a chair.

'No,' her mother agreed. 'I wish we had more Saturdays like it.'

Mandy sighed and sat down opposite her mother. She picked up part of the newspaper and started flicking through it listlessly.

'You look fed up,' Mrs Hope said. 'Everything all right?'

'An Old English sheepdog puppy came in to see Dad. He found out it was completely deaf, poor little thing,' Mandy told her. Her mum was about to reply when the kitchen door opened.

'Ah, any tea left in that pot, Emily?' Adam Hope came into the kitchen peeling off his white coat. He flopped into a chair. 'I trust Mrs Ponsonby left Animal Ark in a happier frame of mind,' he teased his wife. 'I heard all about it from Jean!'

Emily Hope laughed, and handed him a mug of tea. 'I think I managed to convince her that Toby's smell hadn't caused a fit in Pandora. Toby's eye needed rinsing out, but he'll survive!'

Mandy was still thinking about Rush. 'Dad, will that puppy – Rush – be scared of not being able to hear anything?' she asked suddenly.

'I shouldn't think so,' her father replied. 'It's

likely that he was born deaf. He'll think the silence is normal.'

'Mandy was just telling me about this deaf puppy, Adam. Do we know the breeder?' Emily Hope asked.

'It's one of Mrs Merrick's pups,' her husband told her. 'She's meant to be a good breeder. But I'm rather concerned . . . the owner tells me that he didn't see the mother dog with the litter.'

'That's odd, if her reputation is anything to go by,' Mrs Hope remarked. 'She lives over near Walton, doesn't she?'

Adam Hope nodded. 'I think she's a client of Tony Spence's surgery,' he said.

'Why do you think that the rest of the litter might be deaf as well, Dad?' Mandy asked, remembering her father's advice to Mr Taylor to check the dog's littermates.

'Well, the deafness might be genetic,' he replied. 'It could have been passed to Rush from his parents. If that's the case, the rest of them might be deaf too.' He sighed.

'Can a puppy get deafness from its parents?' Mandy was puzzled.

'You know how puppies look like their parents?'

he asked. 'Black dogs have black puppies, for example?'

'Yes.' Mandy frowned. 'It's to do with their genes, isn't it?'

Mandy's mum nodded. 'That's right. A puppy's shape and size – and colour – are all passed on from their mother and father.'

'And deafness can be passed on too?' Mandy said.

'Exactly!' smiled Adam Hope. 'That's why good dog breeders choose the parents of their litters very carefully.'

'That way,' Mrs Hope added, 'they can usually stop any problems being passed on to the puppies. So it might be that Rush is just a very unlucky puppy who happens to be deaf. But it's best to check his brothers and sisters, just in case.'

'The sad thing about a puppy being born deaf is that it needs extra care for the whole of its life. The owners don't always realise what they are taking on. Sometimes people find they can't cope with a dog with a problem – and end up abandoning it.' Mr Hope frowned.

Mandy sighed. She hated the thought of an animal being abandoned, just because it was deaf.

'Cheer up,' said her mum, 'it sounds like that puppy is in safe hands.'

Mandy smiled. 'I know,' she said. 'Mr Taylor wouldn't abandon Rush.'

Her dad picked up the paper. 'So, what are you doing for the rest of the day?' he asked.

Mandy grinned. 'I had a letter in the post this morning.' She jumped up and fetched the brown envelope from the top of the fridge where she'd left it that morning. 'It's from the We Love Animals charity . . .'

'Ah!' said Mrs Hope, grinning. 'It's that time of year again, is it?'

'It is.' Mandy waved the letter at her. 'Look.' She unfolded the piece of paper and began to read: 'Are you an animal lover? We need you to raise money for animals in danger. Animal lovers from all over the country will be holding a variety of fund-raising events to support the We Love Animals campaign. If you would like to be one of them, and if you have a fun, original idea for an event, then why not fill in the form below to register your event? The We Love Animals Fund-raising Day will be on Saturday, July 31st . . .'

'Not far off, then,' Mrs Hope said. 'You've only

got a week or two to think of an idea.'

'I know,' said Mandy. 'And I want to come up with something *really* good again this year!' Mandy gathered up the letter and leaflets and stood up. 'I'll go and ring James.'

'OK,' Mr Hope replied, going back to his paper. 'See you later.'

Mandy Hope and James Hunter,
Animal Ark Veterinary Surgery,
Welford,
WALTON,
North Yorkshire

Two

Mandy had arranged to meet James in Meadow Lane. She heard Blackie panting even before she saw him. As they appeared round the corner, the black Labrador was straining on his lead ahead of James

'Hello, Blackie,' Mandy called. Blackie stopped, his ears pricked, then he bounded forward, tail wagging, nearly pulling James off his feet as he rushed up to welcome her. Mandy bent down and ruffled Blackie's silky ears.

'I brought the letter I told you about,' she told James, handing him the envelope. 'The We Love

Animals day is the Saturday after school closes, so we need to decide what to do right away.'

James grinned, pushing his fringe off his forehead. He looked hot already. 'We'll think of something. Come on, I want to let Blackie off his lead before he pulls my arm off!' he said.

'Let's go towards Manor Farm,' Mandy suggested, pointing to the footpath that led back past Animal Ark towards the Greenaways' home.

'Off you go!' James told Blackie, bending down to unfasten the lead.

Mandy fell into step beside James. Blackie raced along ahead of them. He raised his nose and sniffed at the warm summer air. From time to time he was distracted by the rustling of some small creature in the undergrowth and stopped to cock his head and listen. Watching him reminded Mandy of Rush.

'Someone brought an Old English sheepdog puppy into surgery this morning,' she told James. 'Dad discovered it was deaf.'

'Can your dad operate?' James asked, stopping to ease a stone out of his trainer.

'He says he can't do anything – the poor thing was born that way. Dad thinks it might have inherited the deafness from its parents – it's called inbreeding.'

'Yes, I watched a television programme about that last week,' James said. 'When animals that are closely related to each other breed together, they can pass on any weak genes in the cells of the body . . .'

'I know,' said Mandy.

James was about to continue, when they became aware of a horrible smell. 'Ugh!' James exploded indignantly, as Blackie bounded up to them, happily wagging his tail. The Labrador had gone off to explore under a tree by a hedge and had returned triumphant, coated in a slimy, smelly cowpat. The greenish-brown mess oozed over his shoulder blades and dripped down his front legs.

Mandy doubled over with laughter. 'Blackie! You're revolting!' she cried, covering her nose with her hand. 'James, have you brought any perfume with you?'

'Perfume?' James repeated, wrinkling his freckled nose. 'What are you on about? It's not funny, Mandy! I'll have to bath him again. That's the third time this week!' he said crossly.

'Sorry,' Mandy muttered sympathetically, trying

to suppress her giggles. 'It's just that Mrs Ponsonby brought Toby in with the same complaint this morning. Only it was the fault of a fox, not a cow. Mrs Ponsonby had drenched him in sickly perfume – and got it in his eye. It certainly helped to mask the terrible pong, though.'

James laughed. 'Blackie! You're a monster,' he said heatedly. 'Come on, let's turn back. Are you going to help wash him?'

'Wash him!' Mandy exclaimed, seizing James's sleeve in her excitement. 'That's it!'

'That's what?' James asked, pushing his glasses further up along the bridge of his nose and staring at his best friend. 'Have you gone completely mad?'

'We'll wash dogs! We'll charge people for washing their dogs. We'll make heaps of money for the We Love Animals fund raiser!'

'What a brilliant idea!' James breathed, his eyes shining. 'I've certainly had enough practice since Blackie decided he was going to roll in every disgusting mess in Welford!'

'Oh no,' Mandy said, looking round. 'Blackie's off again. You'd better put him on the lead and we'll take him back to Animal Ark. I'm sure Mum

and Dad will let us use the animal shower.'

But Blackie was off again, squeezing through a gap in the hedgerow that grew along the edge of the path.

'Blackie!' shouted James. The hedge parted. Mandy heard a panting sound as a lolling, dripping pink tongue appeared in the gap. Then the shiny black body of an ecstatic, smelly Blackie squeezed through the hedge and bounded up to James.

'Pooh!' said James in disgust. 'Here, let me put this lead on you.'

Mandy laughed as James tried to attach the lead to Blackie's collar. 'Not much of a walk, was it? Poor Blackie. But we've got loads to do,' she told him. 'Let's go!'

They walked briskly back to Animal Ark, Blackie trotting along at James's heels. The powerful smell of manure rose around him. 'Let's hope,' said James, pinching his nose with his fingers, 'that none of the dogs we wash on the day of the fund raiser has rolled in anything as horrible as this.'

'They'd better not,' Mandy said. 'We won't have a free hand to hold our noses!'

'Maybe we could borrow two of your parents' surgical masks,' James suggested, laughing.

As they turned on to the footpath that would take them back to Animal Ark, Mandy began to run. 'Come on, James,' she urged. 'Hurry up.'

James broke into a run, a delighted Blackie bounding along at his heels. But Mandy was first through the garden door into the kitchen, where she almost collided with her mother.

'Yikes, sorry, Mum. Hi, Dad. Hello, Gran!' Mandy was gasping for breath as she greeted her grandmother. Mandy's grandparents lived in Lilac Cottage, not far from Animal Ark.

'Somebody chasing you, Mandy?' laughed Dorothy Hope, who was buttering toasted teacakes on a large platter.

'Yes, James and Blackie!' Mandy replied, grinning, as James arrived in the kitchen.

'Hmm, something smells good in here,' he remarked, closing the door firmly on his foul-smelling dog. Blackie barked in frustration and scraped at the door.

'Oh, he can come in, James,' said Emily Hope. 'You know Blackie is always welcome.'

'No, he can't,' Mandy announced firmly. 'Not today. He stinks.'

'Not another dog who likes rolling in things?' Mrs Hope enquired, her eyebrows raised.

'Cowpat,' James explained and wrinkled his nose.

'Well, you can put him in the animal shower next door, if you like,' Emily Hope offered, as she set the kitchen table.

'That's what we were hoping,' James said. 'Thanks, Mrs Hope.'

'Mum,' Mandy began, collapsing into a chair, 'James and I have had a brilliant idea. We're going to organise a sponsored dog wash to raise money for the We Love Animals day!' She reached out to take a teacake.

'Hands off!' Gran said sternly, tapping Mandy's fingers with a handy wooden spoon. 'I've not finished buttering them yet!'

'Would you like a cheese sandwich, James?' Mrs Hope held out a plate and James took one. 'That sounds an excellent idea, Mandy. So where are you going to hold this dog wash?'

'We hadn't thought of that,' James admitted, looking at Mandy.

'We'll need a really safe garden,' said Mandy, 'so the dogs can't escape; and a tap close by – and a hosepipe.'

'Blackie hates hosepipes,' James sighed, as the Labrador barked from the other side of the kitchen door.

'Well, you won't be able to do it here at Animal Ark, I'm afraid,' Mrs Hope told them. 'We're usually busy on a Saturday morning and we can't have a bunch of overexcited dogs bounding around upsetting all the patients.'

'I suppose you could use our garden,' said Gran thoughtfully, offering Mandy a teacake. 'But your grandad would have to patch up the holes in the fence first. You can't have dogs escaping into the road! And like Blackie, most dogs aren't too keen on being washed.'

'We'll need two people to do the bathing – one to hold, and one to shampoo and rinse,' Mandy decided.

James brushed the breadcrumbs from round his mouth. 'We'll need someone to take care of the dogs while they wait too. My cousin Jenny's coming to stay at the end of term – she won't mind helping,' he said.

'Perhaps your father would give you a hand too, Mandy,' Mrs Hope said, glancing across at her husband. 'I can cope with the morning surgery, with Simon's help. Maybe Dad can help you to supervise the dogs.'

Adam Hope groaned. 'Just what I need – a garden full of unruly wet dogs to look after . . .' he grumbled playfully.

'Dad!' Mandy scolded him. 'It's for a good cause!'

'All right, then,' Mr Hope grinned. 'You've twisted my arm.'

'Thanks, Dad.' Mandy smiled. She knew that her dad would enjoy the dog wash almost as much as she would.

'Why don't you make some leaflets to put through letterboxes,' Gran advised, pouring out tea for everyone. 'You'll have to make sure everybody knows about it.'

Mandy's eyes were shining. 'Yes! Of course! We'll design some posters and put them up all over Welford. That should attract loads of dog owners.'

'At last,' said James, 'a chance to show off my artistic talent.'

'What artistic talent?' Mandy teased.

'Oh . . . Mandy, this came for you this morning.' Mrs Hope held up a small white envelope. 'I mixed it up with my own mail by mistake. Sorry.'

'Thanks, Mum,' said Mandy, taking the letter from her mother. She studied the postmark. 'Oh, look, it must be from John Hardy. It's addressed to both of us, James!' But before they could open it, they heard an indignant scraping at the kitchen door.

'Poor Blackie,' said Mr Hope. 'You'd better get back to him. He doesn't sound too happy.'

James laughed. 'He really is getting fed up. Come on, Mandy. Let's open that letter outside – or Blackie might just break down the door!'

Mandy sat cross-legged on the springy grass and held Blackie at bay with on outstretched arm.

'Sit!' James commanded. Blackie cocked his head at his master and did as he was told. 'Good boy,' James said. 'Hurry up with that letter, Mandy. We're going to have to bath Blackie. I can't stand the smell much longer.' He pinched his nose.

'It's a very short letter,' Mandy remarked, scanning the small piece of notepaper. 'It just says that he's coming home for the holidays . . . um –'

Mandy found the date she was looking for '– on July 15th – he breaks up before we do. He'll be back here on the 16th.'

'Good,' James said. 'That's great. He'll be here for the fund-raising day.'

John Hardy was eleven years old, the same age as James. He was a boarder at Grange School in the Lake District, but in the holidays he lived with his father Julian and his stepmother Sara at Welford's Fox and Goose pub.

'We'd better write back right away then,' James decided. 'I'm sure he'll want to help with the dog wash.'

'Good idea,' Mandy agreed. 'John will love it – and we're going to need some help.' She got to her feet. 'It looks like we're going to have a busy afternoon. Let's wash Blackie first, then we can write to John. And then we've got to think about a design for our posters . . .'

'Fine by me,' grinned James. 'But do you think I'll have time for one of your gran's toasted teacakes first?'

Mandy and James were about to take Blackie into the residential block for his shower, when Ted

Forrester, the local RSPCA inspector, turned up.

'Hi, Ted,' Mandy smiled.

'Hello, Mandy, James,' he said. He put out a hand to pat Blackie, then quickly withdrew it. 'Uh oh!' he laughed.

'Yes,' James said grimly, 'Horrible, isn't it? We're just taking him into Animal Ark for a shower.'

'I won't keep you, then. I wanted to see your dad, Mandy. Is he busy? Only he rang a while ago about a pup from Mrs Merrick's place.'

'Hello there, Ted. I thought I heard your voice,' Adam Hope called from the kitchen door. 'Thanks for stopping by.' He came outside, squinting in the bright afternoon sun.

'No trouble. Problem?' Ted took off his cap.

'I'm not sure,' Mr Hope said, frowning. 'We had an Old English sheepdog pup come in this morning. I'm pretty certain it was younger than the owner had been led to believe, and stone deaf. The chap said he'd got it from Mrs Merrick. He hadn't seen the puppy with its mother, either. It all seems a bit odd . . .'

'You can say that again,' Ted replied. 'She's got a good name as a breeder, Mrs Merrick has. Of course, it's a hobby for her, rather than a real business. She lives over Walton way.'

'Yes, I know her property. Big iron gates shaped like dogs' heads . . .' Adam Hope said. Then he added, 'Of course, this puppy could have been a throwback, but it's strange that the mother dog was missing. I don't want to go poking my nose in where it's not wanted, Ted. You understand.'

'Don't worry,' Ted reassured him. 'I'll do some nosing around. I'll make it a social call though. I don't want to upset her,' he said.

'Thanks, Ted. That will put my mind at ease.' Adam Hope smiled.

'And mine,' Mandy said quietly.

'Mind you,' Ted Forrester said, 'it won't be for a couple of days yet. I'm run off my feet with work at the moment. I'll get over to her just as soon as I can, all right?' Ted sniffed, then looked around and down at Blackie. 'Now, young James,' he said. 'What about that shower for this smelly dog?'

James pushed his glasses higher up on the bridge of his nose and squared his shoulders. 'Yes,' he said, and turned to Mandy. 'Ready for battle?' he asked.

'As ready as I'll ever be!' she laughed. 'Let's do it!'

'WE LOVE ANIMALS' CHARITY

Put your money
where your heart is.

SPONSORED DOG WASH

SATURDAY 31ˢᵗ JULY
11 A.M.
THE FOX AND GOOSE
WELFORD

Three

Blackie's happily thumping tail drooped suddenly when he spotted the shower. His ears went back. He turned about and tried to slink out of the door, back into the garden.

'Grab him!' James yelled at Mandy, who sprang forward and tucked her fingers firmly through the Labrador's collar.

'Sorry, Blackie,' Mandy said as she led him into the cubicle. 'You might think you smell wonderful, but we don't!'

'Don't look at me like that, Blackie.' James grinned at the mournful expression on Blackie's face. 'You're used to being washed by now.'

James put Blackie under the shower-head and held him there. Mandy turned on the warm spray. Blackie shuddered, then began to shake his fur out. 'Ugh!' cried Mandy, as droplets of dirty water flew in all directions. 'I'm soaked!'

'We'll have to wear raincoats for the dog wash!' James laughed. When Blackie's coat was wet through, Mandy turned off the tap. James squeezed a blob of dog shampoo on to Blackie's shoulders and began to massage it into a lather of bubbles. Mandy helped him, working the soap into a froth around Blackie's neck and down his chest. Blackie looked at her accusingly. His nose twitched from the sharp, clean smell of the shampoo.

'There!' James said triumphantly, when every bit of Blackie's thick, black coat was covered. 'Now, I'll hold him. Turn on the water again, will you?'

'Right,' Mandy said. Blackie shook vigorously as the water cascaded over his shoulders and pooled around his feet. With the palms of his hands, James swept the clean water off the dog's back, leaving his coat standing up in small wet peaks of fur.

'Now you can let him go,' Mandy said. 'The door's open . . .'

Blackie wasted no time in making his escape. He bounded away, then flung himself on to the warm grass outside and rolled, grunting happily, all four legs waving about in the air. Mandy and James sat down on the grass, laughing.

'Just look at him! What a mad dog.' James was grinning, while trying to wipe the water off his glasses with his wet T-shirt.

'He smells much better, though,' Mandy said.

'Hmm,' said James. 'But for how long, I wonder?' He put his glasses back on, then lay back in the sun with his eyes closed.

'Hey!' Mandy poked him in the ribs. 'Don't doze off. We've got work to do, remember?' James ignored her, pretending to be asleep. Blackie, in high spirits, trotted over and peered down at his master. He cocked his head, then licked at James's cheek with his long wet tongue.

James sat up. 'All right, all right,' he grumbled. 'I can't fight both of you. Let's take Blackie home now. We can design the posters at my house. That way, we can use the computer.'

'Great idea,' Mandy said.

Mandy put her head around the kitchen door to tell her mum they were going. Then she and James set off along the lane in the direction of the Hunters' house.

Passing the Fox and Goose, they spotted Mr and Mrs Hardy tidying the window boxes in the front of the low stone building. Sara Hardy, John's stepmother, looked up.

'Hello, you two,' she called. 'Blackie taking you for a walk, is he?' She smiled at the ever-eager Blackie, straining at his lead.

'Hi, Sara,' Mandy said. 'We've already taken him for one walk today – and had to bath him afterwards! Now he thinks he deserves another.'

'Looks like you made a good job of it,' Mr Hardy observed, stroking Blackie's glossy head. 'What a beautiful shiny coat.'

'We've had so much practice bathing dogs that we've decided to make some money out of it,' James told him. 'We're planning a sponsored dog wash to raise money for the We Love Animals day.'

Sara Hardy smiled, easing off her gardening

gloves as she spoke. 'That sounds like a good idea.' Her cheeks were glowing pink in the warm afternoon sun. 'There are certainly plenty of dogs around here, so you'll have lots of customers.'

'We're going to ask John to help us,' Mandy explained. 'We had a letter from him today, saying he'll be back in Welford next week.'

'Oh, I'm sure he'd love to get involved!' Julian Hardy sounded pleased. James tugged at Blackie's lead. The Labrador was nosing about in the pile of soil and weeds the Hardys had collected below the window boxes. Watching Blackie, Mandy spotted a hosepipe coiled beside the open wooden gate that lead into the pub's pretty walled garden. It gave her an idea.

'The only problem is, we haven't found anywhere to hold it yet,' she told Mr and Mrs Hardy. 'We'll need a fairly big garden with a wall around it, so that it's safe. There are too many cars at the surgery and . . .' Mandy frowned.

'Here!' Julian Hardy chimed in. 'This is the obvious place. Why don't you use the garden of the Fox and Goose?'

'Really?' James said, blinking.

'Are you sure?' Mandy asked, her eyes shining. 'That would be brilliant . . .'

'I think it's a wonderful idea,' Sara said, smiling broadly. 'After all, it might give us a few extra customers in the pub, too.'

'Definitely,' Mr Hardy agreed. 'When did you want to hold this dog wash, Mandy?'

'The first Saturday of the holidays,' Mandy told him. She nudged Blackie off her foot, where

he had just sat down with an impatient little sigh.

'No problem,' said Mr Hardy, putting his arm round his wife. 'We'll make that definite then, shall we?'

'Thanks a lot, Mr Hardy!' Mandy was thrilled.

'Yes, thanks, Mr Hardy. This is going to be fantastic.' James grinned. 'Can we tell John that it's going to be held here at the Fox and Goose when we write to him?'

'Why not?' said Mr Hardy, stooping to pick up his gardening tools.

'We'll be off then,' James said, looking at Mandy. Blackie had began to tug James off in the direction of his home.

'Yes. Bye, and thanks again,' Mandy called, hurrying after James as Sara Hardy waved.

'That was good luck!' James said, as they rushed along behind an impatient Blackie.

'Yes, it's great,' Mandy agreed. 'Now, let's get Blackie home and start on those posters.'

James and Mandy designed their poster using James's computer. When the printer had delivered a stack of crisp, coloured copies, Mandy stood back to admire it.

'What a team,' said James, looking proudly at his work.

'It looks great,' Mandy agreed. 'I can't wait to show Mum and Dad. Will you walk back to Animal Ark with me?'

'It's almost suppertime,' James said doubtfully, looking at his watch.

'I'm sure there'll be heaps of food at our house – even enough for you,' Mandy teased. James jumped up.

'Right! I'll just tell my dad I'm going. You bring the posters and I'll see you outside.'

Mandy was right about there being plenty of supper. Mrs Hope had just removed a large, sizzling, cheesy pasta dish from the oven when Mandy and James arrived, carrying the pile of posters.

'You've been busy,' observed Adam Hope, who was slicing tomatoes for a salad.

'I hope you've worked up an appetite,' Mrs Hope said.

'We have!' Mandy told her, stealing a piece of tomato from her dad's salad bowl. 'Can James eat with us?' she asked.

'Yes, of course,' smiled Mrs Hope. 'You're right on time, too.'

'Thanks, Mrs Hope,' James grinned. 'What do you think of our poster?' He plucked one from the top of the pile and held it up for Mandy's parents to see. Emily Hope took off her oven gloves. 'It's a great picture,' she said.

In the middle of the poster, a happy-looking dog was sitting in an old tin bath filled with soap bubbles. Mrs Hope began to read aloud: 'Put your money where your heart is . . . It's a good slogan too,' she said.

'I think you've done very well,' said Mr Hope, squeezing Mandy's shoulder gently.

'And we've had some brilliant luck,' James told them.

'Oh, yes!' said Mandy. 'Mr and Mrs Hardy said we can use the garden of the Fox and Goose for the dog wash!'

'That's decent of them,' Mr Hope remarked.

'Their garden will be ideal for it,' said Emily Hope with a smile.

'I realised it would be perfect when I spotted the hosepipe outside the pub – and then I dropped a couple of hints,' Mandy confessed.

'Hints!' James scoffed, teasingly. 'You were so obvious that even Blackie must have known what you were up to.'

'Well, I hope you didn't make nuisances of yourselves,' Mrs Hope warned sternly.

'No, we didn't,' Mandy protested, making a face at James.

'Well, here's your signed registration form,' said her father, handing her an envelope. 'You can finish filling it in, now you know where you're going to hold the dog wash.'

'Oh, thanks, Dad.' Mandy smiled and put the envelope on the worktop.

'Sit down, everyone,' instructed Mrs Hope, who was spooning out mounds of steaming pasta from the dish. 'And help yourselves to bread and salad.'

'Thanks.' James grinned, sitting down.

'We've only printed out about fifteen posters,' Mandy told her parents as she piled salad on to her plate. 'The printer ran out of paper. Do you think that'll be enough?'

'You could do with some copies to put through doors,' Mr Hope suggested. 'Why don't you pop into the surgery and ask Jean to help you photocopy a few more? She's catching up on her filing this evening. I'm sure she won't mind.'

'Yes, all right,' Mandy said, her mouth full.

'Then we can start delivering them right away,' James suggested.

'Maybe we could take one to that dog breeder – Mrs Merrick, wasn't it?' Mandy said. 'She must know loads of people with dogs. And we might be able to see her puppies while we're there,' she added hopefully.

'Mrs Merrick's house sounds like the perfect place to start, then,' said her dad. 'But finish your supper first, will you?'

As they cleared the plates away, Mrs Hope looked at her daughter. 'Mandy…' she began. Mandy looked at her mother. She spoke quietly but her tone was firm. 'You'll be careful not to mention this business with that puppy – Rush – while you're there, won't you? Remember, it has nothing to do with us. It's between Mr Taylor and Mrs Merrick, OK?'

'I promise.' Mandy squeezed her mother's hand. 'Don't worry!

'OK,' said Mrs Hope. 'Now, don't stay out late, will you?'

'We won't,' promised Mandy, as she headed for the surgery with James.

Jean helped them photocopy a stack of posters and found them some first-class stamps for their envelopes – one letter to John Hardy and the other containing the registration form. Jean offered to post them on her way home.

'I'll take a bunch of these leaflets you've made too, if you like,' she suggested. 'I'll drop them off in letterboxes as I go.'

Although the surgery photocopier had churned out the posters in black and white, and the golden retriever James had drawn no longer looked quite as handsome sitting in his tin bath, they still looked pretty good.

'Very professional,' Jean announced as James held one up for her to see. 'They're really eye-catching. I like the slogan, too.'

Encouraged, Mandy gave her a hug, then headed out of the door with James.

They set off down the road to Walton. As they pedalled along side by side, Mandy said, 'I hope Mrs Merrick *will* let us see her puppies.'

'We don't actually know that she has any,' James observed.

'I suppose not,' said Mandy. 'But I'm hoping the puppy that came into the surgery has some brothers and sisters.'

'They might have all been sold by now,' James pointed out reasonably.

'Then at least we'll see the mother dog,' Mandy said with determination. 'I love Old English sheepdogs – they're so big and friendly. Mr Taylor – that's Rush's owner – told me that they're called sheepdogs because they used to be clipped with the sheep . . .'

'Here . . .' James interrupted, as he slowed his bike to a stop by a corner. 'Mrs Merrick's house is over there,' he said, pointing. 'Look, those are the gates.'

Mandy looked on ahead. She saw two massive wrought-iron gates shaped like the heads of two dogs with pointed noses.

'The gates are very grand,' James said in a small voice.

'Not the house, though,' Mandy whispered. She had dismounted and was looking towards the rather ordinary-looking bungalow behind the dogs' head gates. It sat at the top of a paved sweep of driveway. The paint on the walls and round the windows was peeling in places. It looked rather shabby.

Mandy walked over, unlatched the iron gates, and they went up the drive to the front door. James took a folded leaflet out of his pocket and smoothed it over. Then he knocked boldly on the door.

After a few seconds, Mandy heard someone fumbling with the lock on the inside. Then the door opened, just wide enough for someone to see out. Mandy had a glimpse of a worried-looking face, framed by greying hair.

'Hello!' Mandy said brightly. 'Mrs Merrick? My name is . . .'

'Yes,' the woman replied irritably, opening the door a little wider. 'Who are you?' She seemed worried.

Mandy tried again. 'We're raising money for . . .' she began, speaking clearly and rather loudly, trying to be firm.

'Oh, no . . . Not now,' the woman pleaded. 'I'm so sorry, but I can't give you anything. Some other time, perhaps. Goodbye.'

Mrs Merrick disappeared, slamming the door in their faces. James looked at Mandy, speechless.

'Well!' Mandy said indignantly. 'What do you make of that?'

Four

The days leading up to the end of term were very busy and seemed to go by in a blur as Mandy and James planned for the dog wash. They decided to spread the word about the fund-raising event as far and wide as possible. They put up posters in the waiting-room at Animal Ark, on the school notice-board, in Welford's post office and in the church porch.

When John Hardy had arrived home from school, Mandy and James called round to see him at the Fox and Goose. He was as excited about the dog wash as they were.

'Dad's going to move things about a bit in here on the day,' he told Mandy and James, leading them outside to the large walled garden. 'He's making space for us to wash the dogs near the tap here. We're going to put out extra chairs for the dog owners and there will be umbrellas for shade if it's hot.'

'Let's hope so,' said James. 'We're going to get pretty wet.'

'It doesn't matter,' Mandy told them. 'It's going to be great fun. Let's just hope lots of people turn up.'

'I saw your poster, James,' John said. 'It looks really good.' James's face flushed pink with embarrassment.

'Thanks,' he mumbled.

'Everything's going to plan,' Mandy said happily. 'All we have to hope for now is that it doesn't pour with rain on Saturday!'

The Saturday of the dog wash dawned bright and sunny. When Mandy looked out of the bedroom window, there wasn't a cloud in the sky and she heaved a sigh of relief. A rainy day would have spoilt everything.

Mandy was just clearing away the breakfast dishes when there was a knock at the kitchen door. Mrs Hope answered the door to James, and Blackie bounded into the kitchen. The Labrador seized one of Adam Hope's tennis shoes and paraded about with it in his mouth.

'He's really excited,' James apologised, puffing, as he grabbed at the shoe.

'*He's* excited!' Emily Hope laughed, glancing at Mandy. 'Then it must be infectious.'

James was wearing a pair of shorts and a T-shirt. He held up a plastic carrier bag to show Mandy. 'I brought a change of clothes – in case we get soaked,' he told her.

'Good idea!' she laughed. 'Well, we'd better go. We've got to be ready to start by eleven, and it's ten o'clock now. We'll need time to set things up.'

'I'm ready,' James told her. 'Jenny arrived last night. She's going to meet us there.'

Mandy picked up a carrier bag filled with plastic bottles of dog shampoo. 'Will you make sure Dad comes over in time for the start, Mum?' she asked.

Emily Hope nodded. 'He's got a few things to do in the surgery – but he'll be there. I hope it all goes smoothly. I'll come over as soon as surgery is finished,' she promised. 'Have fun!'

'We will. Thanks,' called Mandy, as the kitchen door slammed loudly behind her.

The garden of the Fox and Goose had been transformed. Mr Hardy had moved the wooden tables, benches and assorted chairs to the far end, leaving plenty of room for a crowd of excited dogs and their owners.

Mandy beamed, looking around at the garden. 'Oh, this is brilliant. Thank you!'

'Well, it's for a good cause,' Sara Hardy smiled, surveying the pile of equipment that James had just dumped on the grass.

'Sara,' John asked, 'can we use that big table in the kitchen to put out here? Don't you think we'll need a table, Mandy?'

'Yes. Someone will have to stand behind it and take the money as people come in,' Mandy agreed. 'Maybe Dad can do that. James has got a big glass jar from his mum to put the money in.'

'Right,' John said, in his best businesslike manner. 'I'll go and get the table. Will you help me, James?'

'OK,' said James. 'Can I leave Blackie loose out here, Mrs Hardy?'

'Yes, he'll be fine in the garden. He can't get out.' Sara Hardy smiled.

'Here's Jenny!' Mandy called, rushing over to meet James's cousin at the gate. They had met when Mandy had gone with James to spend a week's holiday in the Welsh fishing village where Jenny lived.

'Hello, Mandy,' Jenny said, a bit shyly, in her soft Welsh accent. She wore her dark hair in bunches, just as Mandy remembered her.

'Hi, Jenny!' Mandy smiled. 'Thanks for coming. It's great to see you. I'm really glad we've got you to help. Would you mind hanging this sign on the gate for me? It's nearly eleven – time for people to start arriving.'

'Important! Please keep gate closed,' Jenny read. 'OK.' She grinned and hurried off to the gate.

'Mandy!' James said urgently. 'Look! There are people here already.' Mandy looked. A couple she didn't know had come hesitantly through the gate and into the garden. They had a big, hairy mongrel on a lead.

'Are you open yet?' the woman inquired. 'Only,

we were passing and saw your poster . . .'

'Certainly!' grinned Mandy. 'Bring him in. It's three pounds for each dog. What's his name?'

'Mucky,' said the woman, ruffling the dog's coat affectionately. 'And it suits him! He's in need of a good wash, I'm afraid.'

James had taken off his shoes in preparation for a good soaking. 'How does Mucky feel about being washed?' he asked cautiously, taking the mongrel's lead.

'Oh, he loves a bath; don't you, Mucky?' grinned the man.

Mandy was relieved. At least their first customer wouldn't be a tricky one. She spotted her father chatting to Julian Hardy and waved to him. 'Dad! We've got out first customer!'

'Great!' said Mr Hope, smiling. 'Well, get to it, and send them over my way to pay when you're finished, will you?'

In no time at all, the garden was filled with chatting people and excited dogs. Mandy could hardly believe how many people had seen their posters. Welford's dog owners had turned out in force to support them, and there were quite a few strangers among the crowd too.

Mr Markham, the chairman of the parish council, brought his beagle Bunty to be washed, and there was a difficult moment when the beagle tried to frighten Miss Martin's Yorkshire terrier, Snap. Betty Hilder brought a young rescued mongrel from her animal sanctuary, and even Mrs Ponsonby came, with Pandora tucked under her arm and Toby straining on a lead.

Mandy, James, Jenny and John got to work and they soon had an efficient production line going. Pet owners were strolling about with cold drinks in their hands, as they waited for their dogs' turn.

'Sara says my dad's going to give a donation to the fund because of the extra money he made in the pub,' John reported, as he joined Mandy who was rinsing off a corgi called Jack.

'Oh, that's great!' Mandy said gratefully. The dog wash was going to be a huge success.

'Look who's next,' hissed James, above the sound of yapping. Mandy glanced up to see Ernie Bell holding Pandora the Pekinese. Mrs Ponsonby hovered nearby, looking worried. She wore a wide-brimmed straw hat decorated with silk flowers.

'I don't believe it,' Mandy gasped. 'Mrs

Ponsonby is going to let us wash Pandora,'
she whispered.

'Really, Mr Bell . . .' Mrs Ponsonby was
protesting. 'I don't think Pandora will appreciate
the hose one bit. She prefers a bath of warm . . .'

'Now, Mrs Ponsonby,' soothed Ernie,
interrupting her. He stroked Pandora's head and
she panted all the harder. 'I reckon she'll love a
cool shower on a hot day like this. You just leave
her to me. We'll soon have her looking as elegant
as you are. And may I say that's a very handsome
hat you're wearing today, Mrs P?'

'Oh, thank you,' trilled Mrs Ponsonby, smiling

broadly. Then her smile faded and she looked very severe. 'Now, you will take care with my Pandora, won't you?'

Mandy laughed and whispered to the others, 'Ernie's been flattering Mrs Ponsonby. That's how he's persuaded her to let us wash Pandora!' She let go of the corgi's collar and the little dog tore off to find a patch of green grass to roll on.

'You're doing a great job.' Mandy heard Emily Hope's voice and looked up to see her mother smiling down at them.

'Oh, Mum!' said Mandy. 'You got here. It seems to be going really well.'

'Let me give you a tip.' Mrs Hope spoke softly. 'Use just a sponge on Pandora. You don't want to get shampoo in her eyes.'

'No, we don't,' James said, grimacing.

Mandy could just imagine the scene with Mrs Ponsonby if anything happened to Pandora.

The Pekinese submitted meekly to the wet sponge, while Ernie Bell offered advice from a nearby bench. 'Wet her properly!' he urged Mandy. 'Give her a proper bath. She's a dog, not a doll!'

'Ernest Bell!' scolded Mrs Ponsonby, trying to keep Toby from joining in Pandora's bath. 'Pandora doesn't *like* water, I tell you. Don't interfere!'

Two hours later, Mandy had lost count of the number of dogs they had washed. She was hot and tired but she was enjoying herself so much she didn't care. As she looked around the garden, she noticed that there were only a few dogs still waiting for their turn.

'Phew!' gasped James, sitting back on the grass. 'It feels like we've washed every dog in Yorkshire!'

'I think we might have,' said John, passing round the tray of cold drinks that Sara had given him. Mandy took one of the plastic cups and drank gratefully.

'My fingers are numb,' Jenny announced.

'Hmm, mine too,' Mandy said, examining them as she crunched on a piece of ice.

'Just one more to go, everyone,' said Mr Hardy. 'I think that's the lot, after this next little fellow. Every dog in Welford must be squeaky-clean – well done!'

The last dog to be washed was a small, nervous

cocker spaniel. He shook his head vigorously, sending suds of shampoo flying off his long, curly-haired ears. Mandy and James rinsed him off as quickly as possible and gave him back to his owner, who was hovering nearby, holding a towel she had brought with her.

At last, it was over. Mandy sat down in the wet and soapy grass, exhausted. 'That was fun,' she said, grinning at her friends. 'But I'm glad we're finished.'

'Me too,' James sighed. 'I'm soaked through.'

'At least it's a hot day,' Jenny said. 'I wouldn't have fancied getting this wet otherwise.'

'What a team!' John said, patting James on the back. 'We could go into business.'

'No thank you,' James said firmly. 'I feel as if I'll never get rid of the smell of dog shampoo!'

Mandy stood up slowly and stretched. She went to take the notice off the gate. Water from the hose had run down the gently sloping lawn and collected at the wooden gate. The tap had been turned off but it was still trickling under the bottom of the gate and into the carpark beyond.

'Oops,' Mandy muttered to herself. 'I think we've probably flooded Mr Hardy's carpark.' She unlatched the gate and peered out. The water had streamed out and formed an impressive puddle on the uneven surface of the tarred forecourt. As Mandy looked around, she gasped.

A puppy was sitting in a shallow puddle just to the right of her bare feet. Mandy looked down at its miserable little face, and the tangled, shaggy coat. She gathered the little dog gently into her arms. Its feet splayed out with fear as Mandy picked it up. Then, feeling the warmth of her arms, it began to relax against her. The puppy snuggled closer, shivering, and gave a tiny whimper.

'Oh!' Mandy said softly. 'Oh, you poor little thing. What are you doing here? You're only a few weeks old! Where have you come from?'

The pup looked a little bit like Rush, but Mandy could feel the bones through this pup's skin and she remembered the plump, cuddly feel of the well-fed little Rush. This puppy had been neglected. Its fur was matted and its belly was swollen beneath the skinny rib cage – a sign of worms, Mandy remembered.

Mandy felt a hot flush of anger surge through her. 'Who,' she asked the little dog, 'would let you get into this state?' She glared around, peering into the few remaining parked cars, searching for the puppy's owner. There was no one about.

Moving very gently, Mandy carried the little puppy through the gate into the garden. 'James!' she called. 'Come quickly!'

Five

James and the others were clearing up. Mandy saw him wheel round when he heard the urgency in her voice. He hurried over to where she was standing just inside the gate, cradling the shivering puppy protectively.

'What on earth have you got there?' James called, as he came towards her.

'It's an Old English sheepdog puppy,' Mandy said. 'I found it sitting in a puddle outside the gate.'

'All alone? In the carpark?' James asked. 'Any sign of the owner?' He put out a finger and stroked the pup's head lightly. The puppy shrank back and buried its nose in Mandy's forearm.

'No, everyone's gone. Let's go and find my mum and dad,' Mandy said.

'They're over there, in the garden with Mr Hardy,' James told her.

Adam Hope looked up and called out to Mandy as she approached. 'You've done really well – you've collected £105!' he told her.

'Never mind about that, Dad,' Mandy cried. 'Look what I've found!'

Mrs Hope, Sara and Julian Hardy, and John and Jenny, who had been collecting up glasses from the garden, gathered around her. The puppy, alarmed at all the strange faces, squirmed uncomfortably, then edged its way upward and snuggled under Mandy's chin.

'A lost puppy?' Emily Hope frowned in concern. 'Looks in a bit of a mess, doesn't it?'

'Lost – or abandoned,' Mandy said unhappily. 'There's no one around who could own it and it doesn't have a name tag. And look at it, Mum, it's in a terrible state!'

Blackie raised his nose and tried to sniff at the interesting bundle, as Emily Hope lifted the puppy gently from Mandy's arms. 'About twelve or thirteen weeks old, I would guess,' said Mandy's mum. She ran her fingers lightly around the puppy's frail body and looked at the rims of its blue eyes. 'Poor thing! I guess you've been wandering about for a while – you're very thin.' Mrs Hope paused and lifted the puppy to peer at its rather swollen tummy. 'It's a girl,' she told them.

'Oh, it's so sweet,' Jenny said.

'Shall I go and have a look around outside – see if I can spot anyone who might know

something about it?' John asked.

'I've looked,' said Mandy, 'and I'm sure there's no one about.'

Adam Hope took the puppy from his wife, checking its coat for signs of fleas. Mandy stood beside him and James, while Jenny and John hovered nearby, looking worried.

'She might be in need of some liquid if she's a stray. I think we'd better get her to the surgery and have a proper look at her,' Mr Hope said at last.

'Can I come with you?' James asked.

'I'll go with John,' Jenny said. 'We'll see if we can find anyone in the village who knows where she came from.'

'I've got just the name for you,' said Mandy, peering at the little pup. 'We'll call you Puddles.'

Mrs Hope raised her eyebrows. 'Mandy, you know the rules . . .'

Mandy knew she was not supposed to give stray animals names, but she was determined that the defenceless, abandoned puppy should be cared for now. 'She should have a name – that's the least she deserves,' she protested.

'You go on back to Animal Ark,' Sara Hardy

said, putting a hand on Mandy's shoulder. 'Julian and I will finish clearing up here. And if anyone comes looking for a puppy, we'll send them straight over to you.'

Back at the surgery, the puppy seemed more nervous than ever. She wiggled about in Mandy's arms, trying to hide by burying her head. Mandy spoke soothingly to her, and Puddles responded gratefully by licking Mandy's chin.

Adam Hope examined her carefully. 'She needs a good wash, Mandy,' he said. 'She's had tummy trouble and she's rather dehydrated and weak. I'll give her a worming medicine and put her on a drip to get some fluid into her.'

'Can't I feed her, Dad?' Mandy pleaded. 'She's so thin – she must be starving.'

'Not just yet, love. We'll try her on a small amount of food a bit later. Let's see how she responds to the fluid first.'

Mandy stood with James, watching the puppy hunched miserably on the examination table. Puddles hung her head, refusing to look at them. 'How can people be so cruel?' James asked, angrily.

'It never ceases to amaze me, James,' Mr Hope sighed, 'but they can – and they are.'

'This is the second Old English sheepdog puppy in some kind of trouble,' Mandy said.

'You're right, Mandy,' confirmed Mrs Hope, glancing at her husband. 'This puppy would be about the same age as the deaf puppy that came in to see you – Rush, was it?'

'That's right,' said Adam Hope, peering into Puddles' ear. 'Mr Taylor brought Rush in about . . . let's see . . . three weeks ago now. It might be a coincidence, but this pup could easily have been a littermate to little Rush. Luckily, this puppy has perfectly good hearing.'

'It's that Mrs Merrick again!' Mandy declared furiously. 'That woman . . .'

'Hold on, Mandy.' Mrs Hope held up her hand. 'We have no idea whether this poor scrap has anything to do with Mrs Merrick. You can't go around blaming people when we don't have the facts.'

'Well,' Mandy began, 'she breeds Old English sheepdogs, doesn't she?'

'That's no evidence at all,' Adam Hope pointed out gently. 'This puppy may have been abandoned from a car by her owners as they passed through Welford. Or she may have escaped from home. Someone might be going frantic looking for her.'

'It's strange that she turned up at the Fox and Goose just as we were having the dog wash,' James mused.

'Mum, do you think somebody put her out of a car at the pub because they knew there would be dog lovers there?' Mandy asked.

Emily Hope put an arm round Mandy. 'I don't know, love. The main thing is, she's safe with us here now. We'll take care of her.'

There was a soft knocking on the door of the treatment room and Mandy's heart leaped. Was this Puddles' owner come looking for her?

'Only me . . .' Ted Forrester put his head round the door.

'Hello, Ted!' said Mr and Mrs Hope together.

'I stopped in at the Fox and Goose and Mrs Hardy told me about the puppy Mandy found,' Ted told them. 'Anything I can do?'

'We were just discussing how it might have got there, Ted,' Adam Hope said.

'And speculating on whether it might be one of Mrs Merrick's pups...' Emily Hope added.

Ted walked over to the examination table and stooped to look at Puddles. 'Hello there, little un . . .' he began, tipping the little dog's chin up with his finger.

'If it *is* one of Mrs Merrick's litter,' said Mandy heatedly, as Ted crooned and stroked Puddles, 'then she should be ashamed of herself! First breeding a deaf puppy and now . . .'

'Now, Mandy,' Ted said, straightening up and looking at her. 'I know she breeds this type of dog, but we don't *know* it's one of hers, do we?'

'I suppose not . . .' Mandy mumbled. She knew she was being unreasonable but she couldn't help herself. She felt sure that Puddles was something to do with the Merrick kennels.

'Mrs Merrick might have sold this puppy in good faith to someone who decided simply to get rid of it, you know,' Ted continued.

'Have you spoken to Mrs Merrick about Rush, Ted?' Mr Hope asked.

'I can't say that I have,' admitted Ted. 'It's been a hectic time for me lately – but I will, I promise.' He glanced at Mandy. 'But we can't go upsetting the lady, mind, by going around making wild accusations.'

'It's a bit of a strange coincidence,' Mandy insisted.

'Well, never mind about that. Let's get on with sorting out this puppy, shall we?' Emily Hope said briskly, changing the subject. She steered Mandy towards the basin. 'You run some warm water in there, and I'll get some shampoo. We'll clean her up before we do anything else. OK?'

'How's her health?' Ted asked Adam.

'She's had diarrhoea, so she's very dehydrated. I would guess she's been wandering for quite a few days. Being so young, she's lucky to be alive,' Adam replied.

'Well, I'll let my colleagues know. They'll put the word out and maybe an owner will come forward. And I'll also notify the police, shall I? Anyone who's lost a pet is likely to report it to them.' Ted smiled and turned to Mandy and James.

'Thanks, Ted,' Adam Hope said. 'I suppose I'd better be getting back to the Fox and Goose. I've left the money we collected with Julian Hardy.'

'I'll let you get on, then.' Ted waved from the door. 'Good luck with the pup. Bye, all.'

* * *

Mandy had half filled the big stainless steel basin with warm water. Puddles' tiny feet scrabbled frantically as she was lowered into it. Mandy felt sorry for the frightened puppy. 'It has to be done,' Mrs Hope said firmly. 'She'll be a lot happier when we've cleaned up the mess she's made of herself.'

'James? Mandy?' Jenny was calling from the waiting-room. 'Are you here?'

'I'll go,' said James.

'Bring her in here, if you like,' Mrs Hope said.

James was back a moment later, with Jenny and John. They gathered around the basin, looking at the bedraggled little puppy.

'Did you find anyone who knows Puddles?' James asked eagerly.

'Nobody,' Jenny said. 'We asked around – we even knocked on a few doors – but nobody knows anything about her.'

'Most people we asked said to come here – to Animal Ark – for help,' John said.

Mrs Hope washed Puddles as gently as she could. The water turned a murky grey-brown from the dirt in the puppy's coat. With a wad of cotton wool, Mandy wiped away the encrusted muck round Puddles' blue eyes. She gazed up at Mandy trustingly.

'What are you going to do?' Jenny asked.

'The RSPCA knows about her, and they'll let the police know,' Mandy said. 'We'll keep her here with us until she's stronger.'

'Let's hope someone will claim her soon,' Emily Hope said with a smile, reaching into a cupboard nearby for a towel.

On the treatment table, Mandy patted and gently rubbed Puddles until the towel had soaked up almost all the water from her coat.

'She looks like a different dog!' John exclaimed.

It was true. The puppy's dirty, matted fur was now a snowy white. Mrs Hope began to tease out some of the twisted knots of hair, using her fingers to prise them apart.

'She's so tired,' Mandy said, as Puddles rolled over on the towel and began to lick listlessly at one wet paw.

'She needs a good sleep,' Mrs Hope said. Puddles was quickly drying off and her puppy fur had began to fluff out. It was streaked with very dark grey, almost black, and one of her feet was darker still.

'She's so tiny,' Jenny sighed. 'I love her one black sock.'

Mrs Hope gently slipped a syringe into Puddles' front leg. She hardly noticed the needle going in. Emily Hope taped a tiny tube into place, to carry saline solution into Puddles' body. The little puppy looked at her leg curiously, and tried to nibble at the tape.

'Come along, young lady,' said Mandy's mum, lifting the sleepy puppy into her arms. Mandy picked up the plastic bottle that held the saline and followed her mother round the table and toward the door.

'I can see you've done this before!' Jenny said quietly, looking impressed. Mandy grinned, and nodded.

'I get plenty of practice here,' she said.

In Animal Ark's residential unit, Mandy and her mum put Puddles into a small kennel lined with a fleecy rug. Mrs Hope hung the bag of saline on a hook outside the kennel and carefully closed the door. 'We must let her sleep. I'll check on her in a few hours' time,' Emily Hope said. 'Now, what about something to drink and a bite to eat for everyone?'

Mandy didn't feel very hungry. She wanted to stay and comfort the puppy. But Puddles' head had drooped on to her front paws and, as Mandy watched, she sighed deeply as her eyes closed.

'Right,' she said, smiling at her mum. 'That sounds like a good idea.'

Six

The next morning, Mandy ran downstairs and straight out to the residential unit to check on their new patient.

'She's had a good long sleep,' said Mr Hope. 'I've taken her off the drip and, my guess is, she's ready for something to eat.' Mandy gazed in at the little pup. Puddles blinked her blue eyes and looked slowly round her kennel, as if trying to remember where she was. Then she shuffled forward and put her wide, black, button nose up against the wire mesh, trying to sniff at Mandy.

'Can I take her out?' Mandy pleaded.

'I expect she'd like some attention.' Mr Hope grinned. He unlatched the kennel and stood aside. 'There you are . . . I'll go and find her some breakfast!'

Puddles sneezed violently as Mandy put her hands gently round her pink tummy. 'Oops! Bless you!' Mandy said, and lifted Puddles into her arms. The puppy's long fur was as soft as silk. She sniffed at Mandy's chin, then found her finger and began to chew on it with needle-sharp teeth. 'Ouch!' Mandy extracted her finger. 'Here, look what Dad's got for you.'

Adam Hope had spooned some tinned chicken and rice into a bowl. It was a special mix for animals that had been ill. He held it under the puppy's nose. She whimpered and began to squirm in Mandy's arms to get free.

'All right,' Mandy laughed, putting her down. 'Now, don't gobble it all at once or you might choke.'

Puddles ate daintily but hungrily, then licked the bowl clean with a small pink tongue. Then she sat down and licked her lips. Mandy laughed.

'How's she doing?' asked Emily Hope, appearing at the door of the residential unit.

'She's much better this morning, Mum,' Mandy told her happily. 'She's eaten and she seems more cheerful.' She looked at Puddles, who was taking small, hesitant steps around the floor. 'Can she go outside on the grass? She might want to . . . oh! Too late!'

'I'll see to it!' Mrs Hope said.

'I'd offer to help but I haven't had *my* breakfast yet!' Adam Hope grinned. He turned to Mandy. 'The puppy should stay indoors a bit longer, Mandy. I want to be sure that she's free of infection. Oh, and by the way, I've written out a cheque for the money you collected yesterday, so you can post it later.'

'Thanks, Dad,' Mandy said. 'I want to make sure the money gets to the We Love Animals fund as soon as possible.' She waved to Puddles who was having her gums examined by Mrs Hope. 'I'll come and see you later,' she told the puppy.

Adam Hope yawned. 'I'm starving. It's way past my breakfast time. Anyone for scrambled eggs?'

Mandy had just finished washing the last of the breakfast dishes when there was a knock on the kitchen door. It was James.

'Hi, Mandy.' He smiled as he flicked his fringe off his forehead. 'I came to see how that puppy is getting on.'

'Come in,' Mandy said, moving aside to let him in. 'We checked on her this morning and she seems a bit better. But Dad says she has to stay in the kennel for a while.' She sat down on a kitchen chair opposite her friend. 'James, I've been thinking . . .' Mandy folded her arms.

'What about?' James looked at her warily. He took off his glasses and polished them on his sleeve.

'We ought to go back to Mrs Merrick's house,' Mandy said. 'I'm sure these poor puppies are something to do with her. We should see if we can find out anything.'

'How do you mean?' James asked, putting his glasses back on.

'I want to take a look around.' Mandy sounded fierce. 'Someone's got to do *something*.'

'We'd have to be careful. Remember what Ted Forrester said . . .' James began.

'It'll be OK,' Mandy said firmly. 'We can pretend to be interested in buying a puppy and just ask some questions.'

James was doubtful. 'She didn't want to talk to us last time.'

'But she thought we were collecting money. If we say we want to buy a puppy, she'll have to let us in, won't she?' Mandy reasoned.

'I suppose so,' James said, looking worried. Then he brightened. 'I suppose we could tell her about finding Puddles, and see what her reaction is.'

'That's an idea.' Mandy threw the damp tea towel on to the rack. 'We'll go this morning.'

'OK,' James agreed. 'I'll go home and get my bike.'

'Will Jenny want to come with us?' Mandy asked.

James shook his head. 'She's waiting for a phone call from her parents. They're travelling around in Finland on some sort of coastguard business and they promised to ring her this morning,' James explained, following Mandy out into the garden where Emily Hope was watering the roses.

'Hello, James,' she smiled, looking up from her work.

'Hi, Mrs Hope,' James replied.

'Mum,' Mandy began, 'we're going for a bike ride.'

'That sounds like a good idea. It's a lovely day,' Emily Hope said, looking up at the deep blue sky.

'We thought we'd go back over to Mrs Merrick's house and ask if we can see her puppies,' Mandy said casually.

'Well, I suppose there's no harm in asking to see them.' Mrs Hope went back to her pruning. 'But, remember, she may not want you there. Just be careful and don't make a nuisance of yourself, will you?'

'We won't. Promise!' Mandy said. She turned eagerly to James. 'Meet you outside the post office in ten minutes?'

'Right.' James waved as he headed off down the drive.

Mandy's heart was hammering slightly as she knocked on Mrs Merrick's front door.

'Yes? Can I help you?' A girl of about seventeen stood in the doorway. She had a pale, oval face and thick chestnut-coloured hair that hung to her shoulders. Her fingers were looped through the collar of a large adult sheepdog.

'Yes, please,' Mandy smiled. 'Um . . . we

would like to see the puppies.'

'My mother isn't here,' the girl told them. 'She's had to go out. I'm Tracy. Are you interested in buying a puppy?' She frowned, looked past Mandy and James as if expecting to see their parents in the driveway.

'We know that your mother breeds Old English sheepdogs,' Mandy explained. 'We'd love to see them . . .'

'If you've got any pups at the moment,' James put in, nudging Mandy with his elbow. Tracy suddenly smiled. She rubbed her eyes and pushed the hair back off her face with her hands. She let go of the dog, who took a step forward and peered docilely up at Mandy and James through a thick fringe of white fur. Mandy stroked its head. She couldn't see its eyes at all.

'Got any? We've got twelve at the moment,' Tracy told them. 'I'm exhausted looking after them all. You wouldn't believe what hard work they are.' Tracy stepped aside. 'Why don't you come in and take a look?'

'Oh, thank you so much!' Mandy said, relieved. They followed Tracy through the dim interior of the house, into a big kitchen with a tiled floor. A barricade of heavy crates had been used to confine the pups in the utility area. Mandy could hear faint whimpering and scuffling sounds, and a few louder, more determined howls.

'Over here,' Tracy was saying, sliding the heavy boxes to one side. The puppies, seeing the strangers, shrank back, then scampered away to take refuge on a heap of old cushions in a large cardboard box. The box had a large U-shape cut out of one side, so the puppies could hop in and out.

'Oh, look!' Mandy said, delighted with the shaggy pups. 'Aren't they gorgeous?'

Tracy said nothing. She folded her arms across her chest.

'They're great!' James exclaimed, looking at the tangle of pale furry bodies and shining black noses. The puppies peeped out from behind each other and blinked at Mandy and James, but seemed reluctant to come near the strangers.

'Can we touch them?' Mandy asked Tracy. She nodded and yawned.

'Of course. I'm going to make myself a sandwich. I haven't had any breakfast yet and I'm starving. So if you wouldn't mind keeping an eye

on them for me, that would be great,' she said.
'Don't let any escape, for heaven's sake!' She
yawned again.

Mandy noticed shadows under Tracy's eyes.
'Oh, don't worry. We'll take care of them. You
have a break,' Mandy smiled.

A telephone rang in the hallway, and Tracy
sprinted away to answer it. The adult dog lay
down on the kitchen floor and Mandy and James
stepped over into the puppies' enclosure, pulling
the barricade shut behind them. One of the larger
pups gave a fierce little growl and took a step
forward, sniffing at Mandy's outstretched fingers.

'Hello,' Mandy said softly, crouching down to
greet the little dog. 'Come and say hello . . .'
Mandy expected the puppy to jump up at her.
She loved the comical curiosity of puppies, and
the way they responded trustingly to anyone who
was kind to them. But this pup was different. He
and the other pups seemed reluctant to come
near. The puppy turned round and clambered
back into the box over the heads of a few smaller,
sleeping puppies.

'James!' Mandy whispered. 'They don't behave
as they should, do they?'

'How do you mean?' James whispered back. He was kneeling on the newspapers and had just noticed a dark wet patch spreading across the fabric of his jeans. He wrinkled his nose.

'Well, they don't seem playful or interested . . .' Mandy couldn't quite explain what was wrong.

'Probably sleepy,' James said. 'Shh, that girl's coming back.'

Tracy came into the kitchen, her sandals making a little tapping sound on the tiles. She buttered a slice of bread and then hunted about in the fridge for something.

Mandy stood up. 'The pups are all so sweet,' she said to Tracy. 'How on earth do people choose?'

'Do you want a male or female? That's a start,' Tracy said without turning round. She was slicing cheese from a big yellow block. Mandy looked at James, who shrugged at her. 'Um . . . a girl, probably,' Mandy said quickly.

James had started creeping across the expanse of newspaper with his fingers stretched out, trying to coax a tiny puppy forwards. It whimpered, then yawned and toppled over. The adult dog wandered over to the barricade and put its large, square muzzle over the top to look in.

'What an enormous litter!' Mandy said, wondering why the puppies varied in size quite as much as they did. Tracy glanced over her shoulder. 'We've got a mixed bunch here – about four separate litters,' she said, through a mouthful of cheese sandwich. 'Maybe more – I've lost count.'

'What?' Mandy asked. 'Really? How come?' She stood up, frowning.

'Well, my mother does run a business here, you know,' Tracy said sharply. Mandy decided it was best not to ask any more questions. Tracy yawned again and rubbed her eyes. 'Here, Troy. Here, boy!' Tracy called the adult dog to her side.

'Can we help you with the puppies, Tracy?' Mandy asked hopefully. 'I mean, James and I love dogs. We'd love to spend some time helping to feed them, or clean up or something . . . anything.'

'Yes, we really would,' James confirmed. He had pulled a puppy into his lap and was fiddling with its tiny ears.

'Really?' Tracy had brightened. She came over, her sandwich in her hand. 'I could really use some help. They're due for a clean out, as you can probably smell. And feeding them all is a nightmare – some of the little ones are still on bottles.' Then she hesitated. 'I can't pay you, you know.'

'Oh, we don't want any money!' Mandy told her. Then, she asked the question she had been trying to hold back. 'Where is . . . where *are* . . . the mother dogs?'

'Look, I told you,' Tracy said, 'we're running a business here. I've had to give up college to help my mother, you know and . . .'

To Mandy's horror, she saw that Tracy's eyes were wet with tears.

'Right,' said James, getting quickly to his feet. 'Where do you keep the bucket and mop?' he asked. 'Let's make a start.'

'Oh, look, I'm sorry,' Tracy said miserably. 'It's just that I'm tired, really. I didn't mean to snap at you.'

'That's all right,' Mandy smiled. 'We'd like to help. What can we do?'

'You know, we found an Old English sheepdog puppy just like these,' James said suddenly. 'It was wandering outside the Fox and Goose in Welford.'

Tracy, who was delving into a tall cupboard in

search of a bucket, spun round and stared at James. 'Really?' she asked, her eyes wide.

'Yes,' Mandy said in what she hoped was a casual voice. 'It's very young and it was in a terrible state. My mum and dad are vets, and they've been looking after it in the residential unit at Animal Ark.'

'What did it look like?' Tracy asked anxiously.

James looked at Mandy. 'About twelve or thirteen weeks, we think,' Mandy told her. 'But it was very thin and sad-looking – and its coat was in a terrible mess,' Mandy finished.

'One very dark grey foot – the other three white?' Tracy asked, her voice hopeful.

'Yes, that's it. Exactly,' Mandy confirmed.

'Petal!' Tracy breathed, covering her face with her hands. 'Petal! I can't believe it! You *found* her! Is she safe? Is she all right?'

'She is one of your puppies!' Mandy cried. 'She's fine, Tracy,' she added reassuringly. 'Don't worry. She's dehydrated because she's had a tummy upset, so she's a bit weak but…' Mandy stopped. Tracy's thin shoulders were heaving. From behind the hands that covered her face Mandy and James could hear muffled sobs.

Seven

Tracy Merrick was crying noisily. Mandy looked at James in alarm and he shrugged his shoulders. She stepped across the barricade of crates and hurried to Tracy's side. 'Don't cry, Tracy,' she pleaded. 'Puddles – Petal – is safe. What happened to her?'

Tracy sniffed loudly. 'Mum was furious,' she mumbled through her tears. 'It was quite a few days ago, now. I must have left the barricade open and Petal squeezed through. She was the liveliest of the litter. She was always trying to escape and explore. She got out of the kitchen door and I didn't notice. Then, when I went to open the front door . . .'

James put the sheepdog puppy he'd been playing with back on the cushion and joined Mandy and Tracy. Troy, the adult dog, was staring mournfully up at Tracy.

'Well, it's good news that she's safe, isn't it?' Mandy asked, wishing Tracy would stop crying. Her nose had gone very red and her skin was blotchy.

'I suppose so,' Tracy said, sniffing. 'It's just that – well, we've got too many puppies and when mum has to go out . . . I thought . . .' she paused and gasped, covering her face again, 'I thought that Petal was dead! She was my favourite, too.'

'It's OK, Tracy,' Mandy said, soothingly. 'We found her and she's doing fine. You could come and visit her at Animal Ark.' Mandy didn't want Tracy to take Puddles back. Mrs Merrick would only sell the puppy. Tracy had said herself that the puppies were only a business.

Tracy snatched a tissue from a box on a small kitchen table, then sat down with a heavy sigh. She blew her nose loudly, making Troy prick up his ears.

'Yes,' she said wearily. 'I'd like to come and see Petal – as soon as I can get away. Now . . .' Suddenly Tracy sat up straight and businesslike. 'I need to get to work. Mum will be so relieved if everything's done when she gets home.'

'Has she been away for long?' Mandy asked, eyeing the pile of unwashed dishes and the general mess in the kitchen.

'She went out early this morning. She's having problems with the bank,' Tracy confided hesitantly. 'Her bank manager wanted to meet her today to try and sort things out.'

'Shall I fill a bucket and wash this floor?' James suggested helpfully.

'Yes, please. There's one in that cupboard,' Tracy said, pointing. She had stopped crying, Mandy saw with relief. 'Mandy,' she asked, 'would you collect the dirty newspaper and throw it in that bin-bag for me? I'll go and start making up the milk formula.'

When Tracy had gone out of the kitchen, Mandy turned to James. 'No mother dogs!' she hissed. 'That's awful. People are coming here and buying these puppies without having seen them with their mother.'

'Where do you think she's getting all the puppies from, then, if there are no mother dogs here?' James sounded puzzled.

'I don't know,' Mandy told him, frowning. 'But I know my mum and dad wouldn't like it. You're supposed to see pups with their mother when you buy one.'

Mandy stepped gently over the barricade and three plump little puppies shuffled out of her way. In the box, some of the pups were still asleep, snuggled up tightly together with their legs intertwined, so that it was difficult to tell where one pup ended and another began. Mandy longed to pick them up and play with them but, somehow, these puppies didn't seem very interested in playing.

'She's really upset, isn't she? Tracy, I mean,' James observed, dipping his mop into a bucket. 'We'd better not ask her any more questions. She might get upset again.'

'Hmm,' said Mandy, torn between her anger about the motherless puppies and her sympathy for Tracy. 'She said she had to give up college to help her mum out,' she remembered. 'I wonder what happened so that her mum couldn't cope?'

'It does sound strange,' James agreed. Mandy had heaped the soiled newspapers into a pile, clearing an area of floor space for James's mop. The puppies had retreated into the big cardboard box and sat staring out with nervous expressions on their tiny faces.

'Oh, look at them, James!' Mandy sighed, getting down on her knees to look. 'Aren't they great?' An assortment of blue and black eyes looked back solemnly at her. 'I wish I could have one,' she confessed.

The kitchen door squeaked as Tracy came back in carrying two large tins of a puppy milk formula. 'This is Tina,' she announced, as she put the tins down on the worktop. 'She's been snoozing in the sun, haven't you, darling?' Mandy looked up at a very large Old English sheepdog standing at Tracy's side. She had a bright orange beard of hair round her muzzle and her shaggy coat was a pale grey-blue in colour.

'Oh! Hello!' Mandy said to the dog, which towered over her as she kneeled on the floor.

'She's my mum's special dog,' Tracy said. 'She's had quite a few litters in her time. She's a wonderful mum.' James rested the mop in the bucket and went forward with Mandy to pet Tina.

Tracy began measuring the milk powder into a bowl. 'Tina and Troy were show dogs. My mother doesn't show any longer, so they have a quieter life now, really.' Tracy poured warm water from a kettle into a measuring jug.

'They must need a lot of grooming,' James said, running his fingers through Tina's thick coat.

'We comb them out about once a week,' Tracy said, pouring the water on to the milk powder. 'They need regular grooming, or their coats can get very tangled and matted.'

James started mopping the floor. The puppies scampered away into their box, and peeped nervously out from the hole. Mandy watched Tracy making up milk for three bottles. 'These feeding bottles are used for premature babies,' Tracy told her, as she whisked the milk into a froth.

'Doesn't Tina feed any of the puppies herself?' Mandy asked, puzzled.

'None of these are Tina's pups,' Tracy explained. 'The last of her litter had been sold when these came to us. They're all Old English pups but different ages and from different litters.'

Mandy tried not to look horrified. 'Can I feed one of them?' she asked.

'I'll help!' James called. 'I've finished doing the floor.'

'All right,' Tracy agreed. She screwed the tops on to the bottles and handed one to Mandy. It was warm. 'You get started with these. They're for the three very small, dark-coloured pups asleep in the box. I'll make up the food for the older ones.' She smiled suddenly. 'Thanks for helping,' she said.

'We love helping animals, don't we, James?' Mandy said.

James nodded and held out an eager hand for the bottle.

Mandy sat cross-legged on the floor in the clean enclosure, with James beside her. She lifted a puppy on to her lap. It whimpered in protest at having been disturbed from a warm and cosy sleep. Mandy stroked the pup's wrinkled little brow and held the rubbery teat of the bottle to its mouth. The puppy's nose twitched, then, with its eyes still closed, it grabbed on to the teat and began sucking hard. James reached into the big box and gently lifted another puppy.

'Wow,' said James, surprised at the little dog's strength as it began to suck. 'How old are these puppies, Tracy?'

'Not sure . . .' Tracy replied vaguely. 'Those are about four or five weeks, I think. Some are older.' James looked across at Mandy, who was frowning angrily. She knew that puppies weren't supposed to leave their mother until they were at least six weeks old. Surely any breeder ought to know that too.

'They're so cute,' James said quickly. 'Mine's a girl. What's yours, Mandy?' Mandy looked down at the puppy in her lap. It was lying on its back, and pedalling in the air with its front paws, concentrating on drinking up the warm milk as fast as possible. 'Um, let's see . . . it's a boy!' she said.

Tracy was carrying over a series of shallow dishes brimming with minced meat and puppy meal. 'The bigger pups are on four meals a day,' she told them with a small shake of her head. 'Feeding and clearing up, then feeding again . . . it never ends.'

The puppy in Mandy's lap had finished his bottle and was sitting on the floor, licking his lips. He looked up at Mandy with sad dark eyes. She stroked him softly, murmuring, 'Good boy.' The puppy took a wobbly step towards her and climbed over her legs, curling up in the warmth and safety of her lap. He belched softly, then sighed and blinked up at Mandy. Mandy ruffled the silky little head and breathed in the smell of puppy and warm, sweet milk.

'You are a little sweetie,' she whispered. The puppy closed his eyes. Mandy wondered where his mother was.

She looked up at Tracy. 'Did the mothers of all

of these puppies die?' she asked sadly.

Tracy was laying out the puppies' dishes on the floor of the enclosure. As the puppies tumbled forward, eager for food, she separated them into groups of three and encouraged them by pressing on their noses.

'I don't know,' Tracy replied absently. 'We've never seen the mothers. They came to us to be sold on. My mother agreed to take on one litter, as a favour, and we've had nothing but trouble since!'

'Trouble?' Mandy asked, taking the second bottle of milk Tracy offered her. 'What kind of trouble?'

James was frowning at Mandy. 'My puppy has gone to sleep!' he announced, trying to change the subject. 'Do you want to feed the third one, Mandy?' But Mandy only nodded.

'We've been overwhelmed by puppies needing homes,' Tracy confessed, tucking her springy hair behind her ears. 'Mum's having to sell them at less than half the proper price, and it's costing us a fortune to take care of them all.' She sighed crossly and plucked a greedy puppy out of its dish. Then she groaned as it began to trample a gooey mess of meat and meal across the floor.

'I really want to get back to college – but I can't,' Tracy went on. 'Mum can't cope on her own – not with all this lot!'

Mandy thought Tracy was going to cry again, so she said quickly, 'Well, that's those two full of milk. Any more?'

'No more.' Tracy shook her head. 'But, we'll need to put down fresh newspaper in a hurry or they'll begin to make a mess on the floor.'

James leaped to his feet. 'Right!' he said. 'I'll get some. Where do you keep it?'

'Bottom of the broom cupboard,' Tracy told him. 'Thanks.'

'I can fluff up the cushions in the box,' Mandy suggested.

'If you like.' Tracy smiled. Mandy waited while James spread newspapers on the floor, then, very gently, she lifted each of the puppies in turn out of the box. They huddled together on the floor, looking bewildered. Mandy untied the lace on one of her trainers and danced it about in front of the pups. One crept forward to investigate but Mandy couldn't persuade him to have a game.

Eventually Mandy gave up. She shook out the

large cushion in the box, and plumped up the smaller ones. Then she put the younger puppies back into their bed. They snuggled together, making little mewling sounds.

James sighed as he spotted a fresh puddle spreading across the clean newspapers. 'Phew! I see what you mean. It is hard work.' He looked at his watch. 'Mandy, we ought to go home now.'

'Yes.' Mandy stroked each of the pups in turn. 'We'd better.' She glanced at Tracy, who seemed cheerful enough now. She was eating an apple and smiling.

'So which puppy do you want to buy?' she asked. Mandy looked at James in horror, trying to remember exactly what she had said to Tracy earlier that morning.

'Um . . . how much are they?' James said.

'£200 each,' Tracy said, 'but my mum might give you a discount.'

'Oh, that's far more than we could afford to spend,' Mandy said, quickly. 'I'm sorry. I hadn't realised they would be quite so expensive.'

'Pure breeds are always expensive,' Tracy pointed out.

'We'll have to save up,' James shrugged. 'Thanks

for letting us play with them.'

'Thanks for your help. I wish you could come every day,' Tracy sighed.

'We could come again,' Mandy offered at once. 'It's school holidays now. We've got plenty of time. *Can* we come again?'

'Of course!' Tracy laughed. 'If you don't mind working! Come on, I'll show you out.'

K521 FH

Eight

'What a strange way to make money,' James mused, strapping on his helmet. 'I mean, it's like Mrs Merrick has a production line of puppies. Someone keeps churning them out and passing them on to her to sell. It's cruel.'

'It's terrible,' Mandy said heatedly, picking up her bike and following James out through the dogs' head gates. 'How could anyone take those tiny puppies away from their mothers? We've got to do something to stop it.' She shook her hair out of its ponytail. She was hot from work and the cool breeze outside was welcome.

'That girl – Tracy – didn't want to tell us much.' James looked sideways at Mandy. 'You nearly gave us away, asking all those questions!'

'I did not!' she answered indignantly. Mandy checked right and left, then pedalled out across the road to start the hilly two-mile ride back to Welford. James drew level with her on the opposite side.

'Sorry,' he said, glancing sideways at her.

Mandy grinned at him. Then she frowned. 'James, look . . .' She braked and James followed her gaze back towards the bungalow. A white van had pulled on to the pavement outside Mrs Merrick's gates. A man got out, walked around to the back and unlocked the door.

'A delivery man,' James said. 'What about it?'

'Don't make it so obvious that you're looking!' Mandy hissed. One half of the double door was open now; Mandy heard a sound like muffled yapping. 'Can't you hear that noise? It sounds like puppies!' she whispered.

'Are you sure?' James asked.

'Come on.' Mandy was impatient. 'Let's cross back and take a closer look, quickly, before he closes the door.' Mandy pulled out back across the road.

'Hang on . . .' James called, following her. 'I don't think . . .'

'Shh, James,' Mandy pleaded. 'Listen!'

They cycled back towards the van. The driver was absorbed in his task. Bending from the waist, he seemed to be rearranging whatever was inside. As Mandy drew closer, she distinctly heard the sound of something whimpering.

Mandy drew level with the back of the van. 'Good morning!' she called brightly. The man straightened up so quickly that he hit his head on the roof of the van.

'Ouch!' He looked around, frowning. Seeing Mandy and James just behind him, he hastily slammed the door of the van. 'What do you want?' he snarled.

'Um, can you tell us the way to Welford, please?' Mandy was listening for the noises from the van, hoping that James would hear them too. But the whimpering noises had stopped.

'That way,' the man growled, gesturing towards the main road. 'Left.'

'Oh, yes . . . thank you,' Mandy smiled. The driver opened Mrs Merrick's gates, then got back

into the van. He started the engine and turned
into the driveway.

'James!' Mandy whispered urgently. 'He must
be delivering the puppies.'

'We don't know that, Mandy.' James was
doubtful. 'You know what your mum said . . .'

'But we've got to do something! I heard puppies
crying in the back of the van. Come on!'

'We could get ourselves into big trouble,' James
warned her. 'And anyway, what are we going to do
about it? Ask her to stop selling puppies?'

'There's something that's not right, James. You
said so yourself!' Mandy insisted. 'We'll cycle on past
for a bit, then hide our bikes and sneak back. OK?'

James shrugged and nodded.

They propped their bikes against the trunk of
a tree in a leafy thicket set back from the pavement.
Then, hurrying back towards the bungalow, they
took cover among the leafy lower branches of a
big elm growing by the entrance to the driveway.

'There!' Mandy whispered to James. 'We've got
a brilliant view from here. Let's see what happens
now.' James didn't answer. He was crouched close
to the trunk, peering out towards the drive.

The man was leaning on the roof of the van,

writing something in a little notebook. When he had finished, he put his pen in his top pocket, leaned inside the van and hooted the horn, making Mandy jump.

Parp! Parp! Parp!

James covered his ears. 'Why can't he just go and ring the doorbell like everyone else?' he muttered.

Mandy watched as the front door opened. Tracy put her head out, then leaned out to see who was in the drive. The man waved at her and walked forward.

'Hello,' he called. 'Is your mother in?' Mandy saw that Tracy was scowling as she walked towards the van. She was barefoot now, her arms folded across her chest. She tossed her bushy hair out of her face.

'She's out,' Tracy said abruptly, her expression furious.

'That's a shame.' He grinned. 'I'll leave the dogs with you then, OK?' he said.

Mandy nudged James hard in the ribs. 'Dogs!' she hissed. 'Did you hear?' James's eyes were wide with horror.

'More puppies?' Tracy said, looking angrily at

the man. 'I thought my mother told you last time, we can't take any more. I'm not taking them.'

'Ah, there must be a misunderstanding,' the man replied smoothly. 'I've got a lovely litter of Old English pups with me – real little champions in the making, they are,' he wheedled. 'I can't take them anywhere else. I'm going to have to leave them here for your mother.'

'No!' Tracy cried angrily.

'She's brave,' James muttered. 'I don't like the look of him.'

'I don't understand. Why are they taking dogs they don't want?' Mandy whispered. 'What should we do?'

'We can't do anything at the moment.' James was firm. 'Let's stay here and watch. I'm going to memorise his number plate.' James shuffled forward. The man was whistling as he walked back to the van. Mandy and James shrank back into the bushes out of sight.

As soon as he began to rummage around in the van, Mandy pressed forward again to try and get a glimpse of the inside. It was too dark to see clearly, but she could hear the pitiful little yaps of the puppies.

'Make sure you tell your mother she's doing these pups a very good turn by taking them in, won't you,' the man said, smiling at Tracy. 'And I'll be back tomorrow for the money she owes me.' He pulled a small wire cage from the van, swinging it alarmingly as he did so. Three tiny Old English sheepdog puppies slid about inside, yelping as they tried to stay upright.

'No!' Mandy gasped, outraged.

'Shh!' James warned.

'We can't take them, Mr Evans,' Tracy said calmly. 'We don't have room for any more puppies and we can't sell them. We've got too many already. My mother said . . .'

'Now, you listen to *me*, girlie,' the van driver said, in a threatening tone, 'I'm leaving this lot here for you, is that clear? And I'll be back for my money tomorrow.' He put the cage down heavily on the driveway. Mandy saw the puppies flinch and cower as it clattered on to the tarmac.

'This is crazy!' Tracy shouted. 'You just can't do this!' But Mr Evans had climbed back into his van, whistling, and started to rev his engine. He swung the van round noisily and turned out of the drive, then accelerated away down the road.

Mandy stared at James. 'Poor Tracy! We've got to help.' She went to stand up, but James put out a hand to stop her.

'Not now. We don't want Tracy to know we've been snooping on her, do we?' he said. 'Let's get back to Animal Ark and tell your mum and dad.'

Mandy looked out miserably from the cover of the tree. She saw Tracy slowly stoop to lift the little cage and hold it up to her face, peering in at the small bundles of white and black fur inside.

'Poor little things,' they heard Tracy say. 'Come along inside and I'll sort you out.' She sighed deeply, then, closing the gates, she walked wearily up the drive to the front door.

Mandy and James arrived back in Welford late in the afternoon, and pulled up at the green.

'I'll come round with Jenny a bit later, to find out what your mum and dad said,' James told Mandy as he cycled off towards home. Mandy turned down the lane towards Animal Ark.

In the living-room, Mr and Mrs Hope were reading the Sunday papers. 'Here you are!' exclaimed Emily Hope, as Mandy burst into the room.

'We wondered where you had got to,' her dad teased.

But Mandy was bursting with the news. 'I didn't mean to be out so long, but we had to help Tracy with the puppies, and then a man tried to make her take some more...'

'Whoa!' said Adam Hope, looking perplexed. 'Stop, Mandy. Take a deep breath, and start from the beginning. Tracy who?'

Mandy sighed. 'Well . . .' she began, 'Mrs Merrick wasn't at home but her daughter, Tracy, let us into the house to see the puppies. Only the puppies aren't right, they don't want to play. There are twelve of them, all Old English sheepdogs, all from different litters...'

'So,' Mrs Hope said carefully, 'Mrs Merrick keeps more than one breeding bitch in the house?'

'No!' Mandy exclaimed. 'None of these puppies were Tina's – that's the dog she breeds from. Tracy wouldn't tell us how they had got them all, but she said that her mum had taken some as a favour and it had caused nothing but trouble.'

'How old would you say the pups were?' Mr Hope asked.

'All different ages. Some were about eight weeks old, but there were some really tiny ones. Tracy said they were only four or five weeks. James and I fed them with a bottle,' Mandy added.

Mrs Hope looked across at her husband and raised her eyebrows. 'Go on, love,' she said quietly.

'James and I were just leaving,' Mandy said, 'when we saw a man arriving in a van. We hid in the trees, and we heard him try to make Tracy take some more Old English sheepdog puppies, but she wouldn't. So he just left them and drove off!' Mandy blinked as tears pricked her eyes. Mrs Hope got up and sat on the arm of her chair. She put an arm round Mandy's shoulders.

'He said Mrs Merrick owed him money,' Mandy added.

'Oh dear. It sounds like a bit of a mess,' Emily Hope said.

'What can we do, Dad?' Mandy pleaded.

'Strictly speaking, this is none of our business.' Her father was frowning. 'Mrs Merrick isn't even one of my clients, so I really can't interfere.'

'But Ted Forrester could?' Mrs Hope suggested.

'James has got the registration number of the van,' Mandy said. 'He's coming over later.'

'That was good thinking.' Adam Hope grinned. 'When he comes I'll give Ted a ring and see if he knows anything about this van driver. If he's trading in puppies, he might be known to the RSPCA.'

'Why can't we go straight to the police?' Mandy asked.

'What for, Mandy? We don't know that a crime has been committed,' her father explained. 'All we know is what you have seen.'

'Did Tracy Merrick know anything about the puppy you found?' Emily Hope asked.

'Oh, yes!' Mandy replied. 'She's one of their pups. She ran away! Tracy calls her Petal,' she added.

'Well, that's good news,' Mr Hope said. 'That gives us a reason to telephone Mrs Merrick . . . Emily?'

'It does,' she agreed.

'Now?' Mandy asked hopefully.

'Not on a Sunday evening, no,' Mr Hope told her. 'It'll wait until tomorrow.'

'But, Dad,' Mandy said sadly. 'You won't let Puddles – Petal – go back there, will you? It sounds like they're so desperate to sell the puppies that

Petal could end up with anyone!'

Adam Hope shook his head. 'She belongs to Mrs Merrick, Mandy,' he reminded her.

'We'll just have to wait, Mandy,' Mrs Hope said. 'Dad is going to talk to Ted.' She stood up. 'I'm going to make a start on the supper. Why don't you give me a hand.'

Mandy was washing lettuce at the kitchen sink when James and Jenny knocked at the kitchen door.

'Hi,' Mandy said. 'Come in.' Jenny looked serious.

'James told me all about your day. Those poor puppies!' she said.

Mandy nodded. 'Did you bring that number, James?' she asked.

James rummaged in the pocket of his jeans and brought out a scrap of paper. 'Yep,' he said. 'Here it is.'

'I'll just go and give it to Dad,' Mandy said, running off to the living-room to find him.

When she returned, Jenny and James were sitting at the kitchen table. James looked gloomy.

'Cheer up, James,' said Mrs Hope. 'Why don't

you get everyone a cold drink. There's a jug of orange juice in the fridge.'

'Ted's not about at the moment,' said Adam Hope, coming into the kitchen. 'Oh, hello, Jenny. Hi, James.' He joined them at the kitchen table. 'He's off at some meeting in the Lake District,' Mr Hope continued. 'But I've left a message – including the registration number of the van. Well done, James.'

'I'll get those drinks,' James mumbled and went over to fetch some glasses from the cupboard.

Mandy stood up and fetched the orange juice from the fridge. 'I just wish there was something we could do,' she muttered.

'I know,' Jenny exclaimed. 'Why doesn't Mrs Merrick take her puppies down to the pet shop in Welford? I bet they'd sell them for her.'

Mr Hope shook his head. 'That's not quite what we would hope for the puppies, you see, Jenny,' he explained. 'We want to be sure they go to the right sort of home.' Jenny looked disappointed, and Adam went on, 'The first rule of buying a puppy is to see it with the mother dog. That way you can be sure that the puppies you see have had the right start in life. There are people who breed dogs just to make money. That means the mother dogs are kept in cramped, dirty and often unsuitable conditions. And soon after their puppies are born, they are taken away to be sold.'

'But why can't they leave the puppies with the mother until they are old enough to leave her?' Jenny asked, horrified.

'Because tiny pups are much more attractive. They can be sold more easily,' he replied, sighing.

'And, as soon as one litter of pups has been taken away, the mother dog is encouraged to breed another litter – until she is absolutely exhausted,' Mrs Hope added, leaning over to put a large bowl of salad on the table.

'That's awful,' Jenny said.

'Yes, it is,' Mandy agreed dismally.

'The worst thing about this business,' Mr Hope went on, 'is that the puppies are taken long distances from the farms where they are bred. They get put into a van with other puppies, from other mothers, without having had their vaccinations, so infections are easily spread. By the time they get to a pet shop, they can be in a pretty poor state.'

'But why don't the police do something to stop it?' James asked.

'The law on breeding dogs is hard to apply,' Mr Hope said sadly. 'There's not much they can do unless there are obvious signs of cruelty – which there aren't in this case.' A heavy silence fell around the table.

'Well,' James said at last, 'we'd better be getting back for our supper.' He looked at Jenny. She nodded and stood up.

Mandy smiled. 'See you tomorrow?' she asked James and Jenny. 'Meet here?'

'Right,' said James. 'Tomorrow, then. I'll ask John if he wants to come too. Bye.'

When the door had closed Mandy slumped back into the chair.

'Why don't you go and see the puppy in the residential unit?' Emily Hope suggested. 'I bet she'd love a cuddle.'

Mandy brightened. 'Is there time before supper?' she asked.

Mrs Hope nodded. 'Just about. Don't be too long,' she added, with a smile.

'Hello, Puddles!' Mandy called softly. She wasn't used to thinking of the puppy as 'Petal' yet.

Puddles turned and pricked up her small ears.

She put her front feet on the door of her kennel and tried to lick Mandy's hands through the wire. Her little stump of a tail waggled with excitement.

'She seems brighter today,' said Adam Hope, who had followed Mandy into the unit to check on the patients. He lifted the puppy gently and looked at her gums and the rims of her eyes. Then he handed her to Mandy. 'She's recovering quickly.'

Puddles squirmed about happily for a few seconds, licking at Mandy's hands. Mandy smoothed the puppy's silky head. Soon, Puddles climbed into Mandy's arms and sighed, her black button nose buried in the crook of Mandy's elbow.

'You're tired,' Mandy chuckled. She held Puddles for a few more minutes, stroking her gently, then put her back into the kennel. The puppy made herself comfortable on the fleece lining, curling herself into a ball. She blinked sleepy eyes at Mandy.

'Poor Puddles,' Mandy whispered. 'Dad, what will happen to her if she has to go back to Mrs Merrick?'

'We'll just have to wait and see,' said her dad. 'Now, let's go and have supper.'

Nine

The next day, Mandy slept later than usual and arrived in the kitchen just as her mother was pulling on her white coat, ready for morning surgery.

'Morning, love,' Mrs Hope smiled. 'I'm just off. Dad's been called out to help at a calving.' She tied her red hair back in a ponytail and picked up a pile of papers from the kitchen table. 'What are you and James going to do with yourselves today?' she asked.

'Tracy Merrick said yesterday that we could help her with the puppies,' Mandy told her. 'I just hope that man doesn't come back and start bothering her again . . .' Mandy felt a flush of anger, remembering the way Mr Evans had bullied Tracy the day before.

'Well, make sure you keep out of it if he does,' Mrs Hope said. 'Just stick to helping out with the puppies.'

'OK.' Mandy grinned, bending to lace up her trainer. 'But I'm going to visit our own special puppy first. I want to say hello to Puddles.'

'Well, don't forget to have breakfast, will you?' Mrs Hope called, as she went out into the surgery.

In the residential unit, Simon, the veterinary nurse, was giving Puddles her breakfast. He looked up as Mandy came in. 'Hi, Mandy. She enjoys her grub, doesn't she?' he said.

Mandy laughed. 'Yes, there's nothing wrong with her appetite now.' The bridge of the puppy's nose was smeared with puppy food. Mandy kneeled beside her on the floor. 'Slowly,' she told the puppy, gently ruffling her head. 'You'll choke if you eat it like that.'

At the sound of her voice, Puddles paused and looked up. Mandy stroked the little pup and earned a messy lick. 'Yuck.' She giggled. 'You've covered me in gravy now.'

There was a knock at the door and Jean Knox appeared. 'Mandy? James is in the waiting-room – he's looking for you,' she called.

'Right, thanks, Jean,' Mandy said, getting to her feet. 'I'm coming. Bye, Puddles. I'll come and see you later.'

It was only just after nine, and already the waiting-room was filled with animals and their owners. Mandy saw James, Jenny and John waiting for her near the door. Emily Hope was looking at a file of case notes behind the reception desk. She called Mandy over.

'I phoned Mrs Merrick a while ago,' she said. 'I asked her what she wanted to do about the puppy.'

Mandy's heart sank. 'What did she say?' she asked, anxiously.

'She explained that she had her hands full at the moment, so I suggested we keep Petal here – for the time being.' Emily Hope smiled as Mandy let out a sigh of relief. 'Just remember she will have to go back eventually,' she warned.

'I know. Thanks, Mum.' Mandy smiled. 'We're going over there now. OK?'

'OK,' Mrs Hope said. 'But stay out of trouble, for goodness' sake.'

'We will,' Mandy said. 'Promise.'

There was a car parked in the driveway at the Merricks' house, and Mandy suddenly felt nervous. Mrs Merrick must be at home. What if she realised that she was being spied on?

'Here we are,' James said, as he unlatched the gate. They wheeled their bikes up the drive and laid them on the grass. Mandy was about to knock at the door when it swung open.

'I saw you through the window!' Tracy smiled. 'Oh, hello!' She looked from one face to another in surprise. 'You've brought your friends...'

'We'd all like to help,' Mandy explained. 'That is, if you don't mind. We thought Troy and Tina might want a walk – and we could clean up the enclosure and feed the puppies . . .' Mandy trailed off as Mrs Merrick appeared, frowning, at her daughter's shoulder.

'Who is it, Tracy?' Mrs Merrick asked.

'This is Mandy, Mum,' Tracy said. 'Remember, I told you she was here yesterday. And this is James. They've come to help with the puppies, and they've brought their friends, too.'

'I'm James Hunter,' James said politely, 'and this is my cousin Jenny Thomas, and this is John Hardy.'

'Well . . .' Mrs Merrick looked flustered. 'It's very kind of you, I'm sure, but . . .'

'Come in,' Tracy interrupted her mother. 'I could do with the help, and the puppies loved having you to play with.'

Mandy saw Mrs Merrick's steely face soften. She looked tired. There were shadows the colour of bruises around her soft grey eyes and lines of worry on her forehead.

'We love dogs,' Mandy explained. 'We'd really like to see the puppies again.' She looked up into Mrs Merrick's face and gave what she hoped was a winning smile. Mrs Merrick looked tense. Mandy held her breath.

'Come along into the kitchen, then,' Mrs Merrick said at last, standing back from the door. She led the way through the house. Troy and Tina came to sniff at the legs of the visitors and Mandy stooped to pet them.

'We've brought you some good news,' James told Tracy.

'That's right,' said Mandy. 'Puddles – er – Petal – is much better. She's put on weight and her tummy upset has cleared up, too.'

'Yes, isn't it good news! I talked to the vet at the surgery this morning,' Mrs Merrick said, her face relaxing. 'Thank you so much for rescuing her,' she added. 'I was so worried about the poor thing. I shouldn't have left Tracy alone to cope with so many pups, but I really did have to go out to buy their food.'

'Don't get upset, Mum,' Tracy said briskly. 'It was my fault, not yours. Let's just be glad Mandy and James found her.'

Mandy climbed over the barrier to look at the puppies, followed by James and Jenny. 'Oh, wow!' Jenny cried. 'There are so many of them!' She reached out to pick up one of the smaller pups which was struggling to climb out of the box bed.

'We've got another three puppies now,' Tracy said grimly. 'It's going to take ages to feed and groom them all.'

'Well, let's get started then,' Mandy said eagerly. 'What do you want us to do?'

'They'll want their feed, first,' Mrs Merrick said,

glancing at her watch. 'Then perhaps you could help to clean them out.'

'That's a good idea,' Tracy said. 'Let's take them all out into the garden. We can feed them out there and they can get some exercise at the same time. With five of us to watch them, there's no chance of them escaping.'

'Oh, yes,' Mrs Merrick agreed, sounding relieved. 'The fresh air will do them all good.'

'This will be their first time outside,' Tracy smiled. 'So it will be an adventure for them. Come on, let's go.'

They carried the pups outside, two at a time, with Troy and Tina following Mrs Merrick out into the sunshine. The back garden was long and narrow, with a large beech tree at the end that gave plenty of shade. Mandy set her puppies down on the grass in the shade.

The younger pups lay on their tummies, their small legs splayed out, and moved their heads from side to side, sniffing at the unfamiliar environment. Some of the puppies began to whimper, and one started to howl pitifully.

'Oh no!' Jenny said. 'They really don't seem to like it out here!'

'They're just not used to it,' Mrs Merrick told them, raising her voice to make herself heard. 'Sit down with them, all of you . . . that's it. Now, see how they are cuddling up to you? It makes them feel safer.'

Mandy lay down on her side on the grass, her body curved protectively around two of the younger pups. The puppies began to settle down, nosing around in the grass beside her. But Mandy noticed that none of the pups seemed very adventurous.

Jenny was sitting cross-legged in the sun with

one of the puppies in her lap. It cowered there, peering out uncertainly.

'Oh, they are wonderful,' Jenny breathed. 'Do you only keep Old English sheepdogs?' she asked Mrs Merrick.

'Yes, I've had them for years. They're a lovely breed.' She smiled. 'They're all born black and white, then, as they grow, their coats turn a silvery grey.' She bent down to stroke one of the pups that had ventured up to inspect her shoe.

'Right,' said Tracy, easing a puppy off her lap. 'I think I'll go and make up the feed, now.'

'Thanks, Tracy,' Mrs Merrick said. 'But I'll do it, if you like.'

'No, Mum,' Tracy said firmly. 'You sit down for a while and have a break. I'll be fine.' Tracy stroked Troy's woolly head and headed back into the house. Tina ambled after her.

As they sat on the lawn enjoying the sunshine, some of the older puppies grew more inquisitive and began to wander further afield. Mandy was just retrieving one of the older pups from a rose bed when Tracy appeared at the door. 'Time for lunch,' she called, walking towards them across the grass with a big feed bowl in each hand.

'Can you fetch the other bowl from the kitchen for me, Mandy?' she asked. 'Oh, and bring the milk bottles too, please . . .'

'I'll help you,' said Mrs Merrick, getting up. 'Come on, Mandy.' Mandy followed Mrs Merrick up to the house. 'It's very kind of you to help us like this, dear,' she said as she collected up the milk bottles. 'You must tell me all about how you found Petal. We were so worried . . .'

Mrs Merrick trailed off, distracted by a knock at the front door. Mandy saw her glance apprehensively towards the hallway. 'Oh, no!' she muttered. 'It's that awful man again.' There was another knock, and she hurried out of the kitchen and into the hall. Mandy began to load the puppies' milk bottles on to a tray she found lying on the kitchen table.

'Good morning, Mrs Merrick,' she heard a man's voice say. 'Good to see you again . . .' Mandy was sure she recognised the voice of the man who had delivered the puppies to Tracy the day before. She stood still and listened.

'Now, Mr Evans,' she heard Mrs Merrick say in an exasperated tone, 'I thought I told you that I couldn't accept any more dogs. You had no business leaving those puppies with my daughter.'

'I've come about the money,' he said, ignoring her remark. 'They're a hundred and fifty pounds each. That's what you owe me.' Mandy crept closer to the kitchen door and peered into the hallway. She saw the driver of the van. He was standing in the doorway with his arms folded across his chest, and one foot on the step inside the front door.

'I don't *want* any more puppies! Can't you understand? I'm not paying for them. You had no right to leave them here,' Mrs Merrick was saying.

'What I understand is that you owe me money,' he smiled, but there was something threatening about the way he loomed over her.

Mandy was furious. The man was obviously trying to frighten Mrs Merrick.

'We had a deal, lady,' Evans snarled.

'No,' Mrs Merrick said firmly. 'We had no deal. You persuaded me to take on the first litter as a favour. You said your cousin was sick and couldn't look after them – you didn't say anything about the rest of these puppies.'

'I sold them to you for a good price,' Evans argued. 'They're worth £350 at least.'

'Yes,' Mrs Merrick sounded angry, 'and I paid

you for the second litter you brought me, and the third litter – but I won't pay for any more. I don't want them. I can't take any more dogs. There aren't enough buyers in the area and I can't find homes for them all. You *must* take them away or else…'

'Or else what?' he sneered, leaning further forwards in the doorway. Mandy drew back, hiding herself behind the kitchen door.

'I'll go to the police!' Mrs Merrick told him triumphantly.

Evans roared with laughter. Mandy was shaking with rage. She was about to run out into the hall when she heard James's voice behind her. 'Where are those bottles, Mandy? The puppies are hungry and . . .'

'Shh!' Mandy frantically gestured for him to be quiet. 'Come and listen to this,' she whispered.

'What?' James said. 'What is it?'

'Listen!' Mandy urged.

'What are the police going to say about you buying and selling dogs without a proper licence? That's what I want to know!' Evans laughed again, as though it were the best joke he'd ever heard. Mandy was on the point of springing forward, but James held her back.

'Don't, Mandy!' he whispered. Mandy hesitated. Mrs Merrick needed some support. Mr Evans's foot was still jammed in the doorway, stopping her from being able to close the door in his face.

'He's trying to make her pay for the puppies he brought yesterday,' Mandy whispered to James. 'She told him to take them back and he threatened her.'

'Now, let's not be hasty here, shall we?' Mr Evans was saying, soothingly. 'You've done these pups a big favour. What would've happened to them otherwise? Now, I've got another pair in the van today, as it happens. Champs in the making, they are . . .'

'No!' shouted Mrs Merrick. 'Absolutely not, do you hear me?'

'All right, all right, keep your hair on,' he said. 'It's a shame, though. If you don't take them, I can't be responsible for what happens to them . . .'

Mrs Merrick's resolve crumbled when she heard Evans's threat. 'Oh! You wouldn't,' she said tearfully. 'You wouldn't put them down, you can't . . .'

'Well, if you won't take the poor little things in

. . . I mean, they've been in the back of the van all night long. They need feeding. I can't keep them much longer,' he said, shrugging his shoulders.

'I'll take them!' Mrs Merrick cried. 'You can't just abandon them.'

'Now, that's what I like to hear,' Evans said, chuckling. 'I'll want payment, though. I'll tell you what, you go and get me my money. I'll bring the puppies out of the van, all right?' Evans finally stepped back from the doorway and walked towards his van.

Mrs Merrick turned. Mandy could see tears running down her cheeks. Mandy stepped out into the hall to meet her. 'You *can't* let that man bully you,' she pleaded. 'Can't we get the police?'

Mrs Merrick looked shocked. 'No!' she said, sounding horrified. 'I have to sort this out myself. The police wouldn't understand. This could ruin me. If it got out what I'd been doing . . . I don't know how I have managed to get so caught up in this dreadful business.'

'What's wrong, Mum?' Tracy had come in through the kitchen. She looked at her mother, then at Mandy. 'What's happened?' she demanded. 'What's going on?'

'That man came again, and he's making your mum take another two puppies,' Mandy replied angrily.

'Evans?' Tracy asked. Mrs Merrick nodded miserably. 'No!' Tracy was horrified. 'No more, Mum!' she begged. 'We can't look after any more.'

Mrs Merrick shook her head. 'What can I do?' she asked helplessly. Tracy put her arm round her mother's shoulders and led her back into the kitchen. Mandy and James exchanged glances, unsure of what to do.

'Will you two go and help Jenny, please?' Tracy asked them, taking charge. 'I've left her and John alone with all the pups. I think you'd better bring them back inside.' She turned to her mother. 'Sit down, Mum,' she urged. 'Let's try and think what to do.'

Mandy and James ran down the garden to where Jenny and John were trying to keep all the puppies in one place.

'Where did you all go?' Jenny asked, puzzled.

'Sorry,' Mandy said. 'That horrible man has come back – with more puppies.'

'Oh, poor Mrs Merrick,' Jenny breathed.

'And poor puppies!' said Mandy, grimly.

'We've got to take them back inside,' James told Jenny, picking up a puppy in each arm.

They gently carried the puppies back inside to their enclosure in the kitchen.

'Can we give them their bottles?' Jenny asked. 'They must be hungry.'

'The milk might need warming again,' James said. 'We'd better ask first.'

'I wonder if . . .' Mandy began, then stopped. She could hear shouting. It sounded as if Tracy was in trouble.

Ten

Mandy leaped over the puppy barricade and sprinted down the hall. The front door was wide open but there was no one in sight. She could hear angry voices coming from outside. James gave Mandy a little shove from behind.

'Come on!' he said. 'Quick.'

'Do you think we should?' Jenny asked anxiously.

But Mandy was determined. 'We might be able to help,' she said, heading for the door.

Mrs Merrick was facing a furious Steve Evans through the bars of the gates. Tracy was leaning against the gates, stopping him from opening them.

'You stay out of this, miss,' Evans was snarling. 'You don't want to get hurt, do you?'

'Let him come in, Tracy,' Mrs Merrick pleaded. 'I'll pay for the puppies this time – but they must be the last. Is that clear?'

'Don't pay him, Mum! We can't afford it,' Tracy shouted. 'This is blackmail.'

Mandy's heart was hammering. She and James raced down the drive to Mrs Merrick with John and Jenny following them.

'Just give me the money you owe me for yesterday's puppies, and for these two I've got here,' Evans said, kicking the cage by his feet. The two puppies whined. 'Then, I'll go – and you can give these two a nice drink of water. They haven't had a drink for a long time.' Mandy gasped in horror. It was such a hot day – had Evans really had those puppies in his van all morning without water?

Tracy, however, was obviously determined not to give in. 'Just take your puppies and go!' she shouted. 'Leave us alone.'

Evans picked up the wire cage with the puppies.

'Well, it looks like nobody wants you,' he said, letting the cage fall to the ground with a clatter.

'No!' cried Mandy.

The puppies yelped in distress and Mrs Merrick could stand it no longer. 'Let him *in*, Tracy,' she commanded. 'Those puppies are terrified. Let him have the money – as long as he'll go!' Tracy was beaten. She stepped aside. Evans pushed the gates open at once and stooped to pick up the puppies. He handed the cage to Mrs Merrick.

'There, now you're being sensible.' He smiled. 'Just give me my money, and I'll be off.' Mrs Merrick murmured something soothing to the puppies and put them gently on the grass in the shade of a tree.

Evans was hovering close behind her. 'My money . . .' he repeated.

Mandy was trembling with anger and frustration. Surely there must be something they could do? Then, suddenly, she spotted the keys to Evans's van dangling from the lock of the double doors at the back. She nudged James and nodded at where the keys hung, glinting in the sun. James gave a small nod.

As Steve Evans followed Mrs Merrick towards

the front door, Mandy slipped out of the gate. She plucked the keys from the lock and darted back on to the drive, passing the keys to James, who put them in the pocket of his jeans.

'Thank you very much,' Evans chuckled, as he counted his money. 'I'll be on my way now.'

'Don't come back,' Tracy called as he strode out of the gates towards his van. He went to close the back doors and, finding the keys missing, checked inside the driver's door. Mandy and James watched as he felt in his pockets.

'My keys,' he said, 'the keys to my van . . .Where are they?'

Mandy gazed back at him innocently, wondering how she was going to get inside to call the police. James shrugged.

'You'd better not be playing games with me,' Evans growled. He looked about on the floor of the van.

'Tracy,' Mrs Merrick said, 'let's get these puppies inside and get them some water.' She lifted the cage, then paused as they heard the noise of an engine. A Land-rover turned into the close and pulled up alongside Evans's van.

'James, look,' Mandy whispered. 'It's Ted Forrester.'

'Just in time,' James sighed, running to the gate.

'Ted!' Mandy called, as the RSPCA inspector clambered out and walked up the drive.

Ted Forrester looked puzzled. 'Hello, you two,' he said. 'I wasn't expecting to see you here. Hello, Mrs Merrick.'

Mrs Merrick looked confused, but Mandy pointed towards the van. Evans had disappeared from view. Ted walked over to the van and rapped on the passenger side window.

'Mr Evans, isn't it?' he called. 'I notice your van's open at the back. Do you mind if I take a look inside?' The driver's door opened and Evans jumped out.

'Yes I do mind,' he protested. 'It's none of your business what I've got in my van,' he said, his lip curling. Evans didn't look so confident now, Mandy thought, noticing the sweat running down his face. Ted walked calmly around to the back of the van. He gave a long, low whistle.

'And what have we here!' he said. 'Puppies . . . Yorkshire terriers, a springer spaniel . . . Very hot in this van for dogs, Mr Evans. I can't allow this, you know. It's causing unnecessary suffering, and that means I shall have to impound these dogs.'

'You've got nothing on me,' Evans sneered. 'These dogs are my property and you can just leave them alone.'

Ted looked unconcerned. 'Perhaps you'd like to complain to the police?' He gestured to the police car that had just pulled up behind the Land-rover. 'I'm sure they'll be pleased to sort this out for us . . .'

Mrs Merrick had been watching in disbelief. Now she walked towards the van. 'Mr Forrester?' she asked meekly.

Ted smiled. 'You remember me, don't you – we met at the Working Dog Trials a couple of years ago?'

Mrs Merrick nodded silently. Tracy stepped up, carrying the cage with the two puppies. 'These are his puppies,' she said, pointing at Evans. 'He's been forcing Mum to take them!'

'Has he now?' said Ted, turning back to Evans.

With his back up against the driver's door of his van, and no keys, Evans was cornered. He looked from Ted to Tracy and then back. Then, pushing past them both, he shoved Tracy out of the way as he headed back towards the drive. 'Ouch!' said Tracy, startled.

'Stop him!' yelled Mandy, as Evans hurled himself back through the gate.

James gave chase with Mandy hot on his heels.

Evans ran round the side of Mrs Merrick's house, scrambling over a small wooden side gate. Mandy pressed the latch, shoved at the gate and followed.

Evans burst round the corner of the house and began to run for the tree at the bottom of the garden.

'Mandy,' James panted, 'if he gets over the fence we've lost him! There are fields on the other side.'

Suddenly, the garden was filled with a volley of angry barking. Troy, who had been dozing in the shade of a tree, had woken up and was now chasing the intruder across the grass. He rushed toward him and lunged for Evans's ankle. Mandy heard the sound of jeans ripping.

Evans lost his balance and fell with a thud, landing heavily on his shoulder. He lay on the grass, unable to get up. Troy stood over him, snarling threateningly as Mandy and James skidded to a halt beside him.

Ted arrived just behind them, with a police officer Mandy recognised as one of the Walton wildlife team.

Steve Evans lay on the ground groaning, nursing his injured shoulder. The policeman crouched down and slipped a pair of handcuffs round Evans's wrists. 'We've been talking to your friends in Wales, Mr Evans, and we think you've got some explaining to do,' he announced, as he helped Evans to his feet and led him back towards the police car.

James, who was bent over trying to catch his breath, looked up at Mandy and grinned. 'We did it,' he said.

'What will happen to Mr Evans?' Mandy asked Ted Forrester. They were sitting round the table in Mrs Merrick's kitchen. Tracy was pouring the tea while Jenny handed round glasses of orange squash.

'We'll prosecute him for causing unnecessary suffering,' Ted said, taking a cup from Tracy. 'And for breaking just about every other rule in the book. The RSPCA has been investigating a farm in Wales for a while – now we have plenty of evidence.'

'But how did you know he was here?' Mrs Merrick asked timidly. Her hand strayed to Troy's fluffy head. He was lying peacefully at her feet.

'Well, it was young James's quick thinking,' Ted explained, grinning.

'Mine?' said James, puzzled. 'How?'

'You took the registration number of the van. Adam Hope gave it to me and I passed it on to Welford police station,' Ted explained. 'We ran the number through the computer and came up with the link to a Welsh farm. And after what you told your dad, Mandy, about Evans trying to intimidate Tracy, we thought we'd better come up here right away.'

'I can't believe how stupid I've been,' Mrs Merrick sighed, shaking her head. 'I should never have let myself get involved in such an awful business.'

'How did you meet Steve Evans, Mrs Merrick?' Ted asked, taking a sip of his tea.

Mrs Merrick sighed. 'At a dog show in Harrogate. He saw my dogs, Troy and Tina, and told me he had a cousin in Wales whose Old English sheepdog had just whelped. A litter of nine, he said.'

'And he wanted you to take them?' asked Ted.

Mrs Merrick nodded. 'He said his cousin was sick and couldn't keep the pups. He persuaded me to buy them. Tina didn't have a litter to care for, so he sold them to me at a reasonable price,' she admitted.

'Mum gave him the money for the litter and we didn't expect to see him again,' Tracy explained.

'Go on,' said Ted.

Mrs Merrick continued. 'Well, then he came back. He brought another litter – six beautiful pups. I'd already sold two from the first litter, but I didn't want to take any more, and I couldn't understand how his cousin had another litter so soon.' She sniffed. 'And, of course, he wanted a lot more money for them.'

'He told Mum he'd put the puppies down if she didn't take them,' Tracy said angrily.

'I knew there was something suspicious about the way he kept turning up with these Old English sheepdogs. And I knew they had been taken from their mothers too young, but they were so tiny – and some weren't well looked after. I couldn't turn them away.'

'Mum was too frightened to go to the police –

or the RSPCA,' Tracy explained. 'Evans had pointed out that she didn't have a licence to buy and sell puppies. She was just trying to help, but he told her she had already broken the law.' Mrs Merrick burst into tears. 'I was terrified people might find out what I'd done,' she confessed.

'But you were trying to help,' Mandy cried. 'It's not your fault.'

'You looked after the puppies when no one else would,' Jenny added.

'I suppose I'm in trouble with the police, too,' Mrs Merrick went on miserably.

Ted Forrester smiled. 'I suspect that the police will be satisfied with catching Mr Evans. Let's hope they can get you some of your money back.'

Mrs Merrick sighed with relief. 'Mr Forrester, we still have fourteen puppies. I don't suppose you know of anybody who could take one?'

'I think the best thing,' Ted said, 'is for the RSPCA to take all the pups into our kennels. We'll find them good homes.' He stood up. 'Well, I'd better be off. Thanks for the tea.' He looked at Mandy, James, John and Jenny. 'I should think you ought to be getting home too,' he said.

Mandy grinned, and stood up to go.

'Um, Mr Forrester . . .' James asked. 'What shall I do with these?' He delved in his pocket and handed over the keys to Evans's van.

'I thought I told you to stay out of trouble!' exclaimed Emily Hope, when Mandy had reported the events of the day.

'What a team,' said Mr Hope, shaking his head. 'It was good thinking to pinch Evans's keys.' He laughed at the thought of Evans desperately searching for his keys.

They were in the kitchen at Animal Ark. Mrs Hope had laid out a wonderful spread of sandwiches, crisps and fruit on the table for lunch.

'Troy was wonderful,' Mandy told her mum. 'You should have seen him bring Mr Evans down!'

'We never gave Troy and Tina their walk,' Jenny remembered, sounding rather disappointed.

'I've got a feeling you'll be seeing Mrs Merrick and her dogs again before the end of your stay here, Jenny,' Mrs Hope said, taking a sip of tea. As she did so, the telephone rang. Emily Hope got up to answer it.

'Hello? Oh, I see. Yes, just a minute please.' Mrs Hope was smiling as she turned. 'It's for you,

Mandy. It's a reporter from the *Walton Gazette*.'

Mandy leaped out of her chair and ran to take the receiver.

'Hello? This is Mandy Hope,' she said. 'The dog wash? Oh yes. Yes, tomorrow will be fine. Thank you. OK. Bye.'

Mandy put down the phone.

'Well?' asked James, excitedly.

'They want to interview us for an article about the dog wash,' Mandy announced, grinning. 'And they want to take a photograph.'

'Fame at last!' James exclaimed.

'Idiot!' Mandy laughed.

Adam Hope put his head round the door. 'Hey! Sherlock Holmes? Dr Watson?' Mandy and James looked up.

'Oh, hi, Dad,' Mandy said.

'Mrs Merrick has just telephoned the surgery. She and her daughter want to take Petal home tomorrow. She said they want to give her the best life they can to make up for the horrible start. I thought you'd like to know.'

James looked at Mandy. 'We can visit her there,' he said.

'Yes,' said Mandy. 'I'm sure we can. And she'll

have a wonderful life with Mrs Merrick and Tracy.' She took a last bite of her sandwich. 'It's all ended perfectly for our little puppy in a puddle after all.'

Puppies
in the
Pantry

Puppies in the Pantry

**Special thanks to C.J. Hall, B.Vet.Med., M.R.C.V.S., for reviewing
the veterinary information contained in this book.**

Animal Ark is a trademark of Working Partners Limited
Text copyright © 1999 Working Partners Limited
Created by by Ben M. Baglio
Illustrations copyright © 1994 Shelagh McNicholas

First published as a single volume in Great Britain in 1994
by Knight Books

To Sue Welford

One

'How exciting!' said Mandy's mum, Emily Hope. 'They're going to make a film at Bleakfell Hall.'

Mrs Hope was busily reading the morning's mail over breakfast. She stuffed the letter back in its envelope. Breakfast at the Hopes' busy veterinary practice, Animal Ark, was always a hurried affair. Fruit juice, cereal, low-fat yoghurt lately as Mr Hope was on a diet . . . toast if you were lucky. All eaten at a huge old pine table in their oak-beamed cottage kitchen.

Mandy dragged her eyes away from her last-minute revision for a biology test that morning.

Mrs Hope took a final mouthful of juice and rose from the table. 'We've been asked to check out the animals they're using,' she said.

Mandy's father looked up from his newspaper. 'Bleakfell Hall, eh? That'll be interesting.' He stroked his dark beard thoughtfully. 'Mixing with the film stars. Don't let it go to your head, Emily!'

Mandy felt a flutter of excitement in her stomach. That would be a real event for the sleepy village of Welford. Famous film stars in their midst! Her friend James Hunter would be excited too, although she knew he really preferred football to films.

'What kind of film are they making, Mum?' Mandy tucked a strand of blonde hair behind her ear. Her blue eyes sparkled. 'One about animals?'

Emily Hope smiled. 'Trust you to think of that, Mandy.' She stood in front of the mirror, ran a comb hurriedly through her long, red hair then tied it back with a green silk scarf. 'Apparently it's a Victorian murder mystery.'

'Wow! Bleakfell Hall's just the place then. I've always thought it kind of spooky. Hear that, Jess?'

Jess, a small Jack Russell terrier, sat at Mandy's feet. Mandy fed her a piece of toast secretly. One huge gulp and it was gone. The terrier gave a little 'woof'.

'Don't think I didn't see that, Mandy.' Mr Hope had a kindly twinkle in his eye. 'She's getting quite podgy. What's Auntie Mary going to say if she comes back from Australia and Jess has put on a stone in weight?'

Mandy giggled. She had been delighted when her Aunt Mary had asked the Hopes to look after Jess for a couple of months while she went to Australia on a university course.

'You know I can't resist those brown eyes, Dad.' Mandy bent to give the little dog an affectionate hug.

'You can't resist any animal that crosses your path,' Mr Hope said.

Mandy grinned. She scratched Jess behind the ear. 'You love toast, don't you, Jess?' Having the terrier to stay at Animal Ark was like heaven to Mandy.

Since turning twelve, Mandy Hope had been allowed to help out at her parents' veterinary practice, Animal Ark, in the pretty Yorkshire village of Welford. Mandy cleaned out cages, helped comfort sick animals . . . nothing was too much trouble. Mandy just couldn't wait to grow up and become a vet herself!

'Well?' Adam Hope looked expectantly at his wife. 'Come on, spill the beans. What animals are they using for the film? Chimps, elephants . . . ?'

'That would be *really* great!' Mandy swallowed her last mouthful of toast and rose from the table.

Dad was teasing of course. Even if it was only cats and dogs Mandy thought it would be brilliant to go and see them. She might even get to see a real film star in the process!

Mrs Hope laughed. 'I don't know exactly. The letter didn't say very much. Just that the animals are being supplied by an agency called Animal Stars and that the company will hire horses from the local stables. They've all got to be vetted before they use them. And . . . oh, yes . . . they mention a dog. Apparently it's one of the stars of the film.'

'What kind of a dog?' Mandy asked.

Her mother shook her head. 'I don't know. Sorry, Mandy.'

'Perhaps it's a mystery dog?' Mandy's

imagination began to run away with her. 'Like in that Sherlock Holmes story: *The Hound of the Baskervilles.*'

Mrs Hope gave her daughter a quick hug. 'You'll just have to be patient, Mandy. They're not coming until Monday.' She dropped a kiss on top of her head. 'As it's half-term you can come up with me if you like.'

'Mum, that would be brilliant!' Mandy exclaimed.

Mrs Hope glanced at the clock. 'Got to rush,' she said. 'Time I opened the surgery.'

Mandy could hear a puppy's excited yelp from the waiting-room of the vet's extension attached to the back of the old stone cottage. She would have loved to go and see the puppy but there was no time. School and the dreaded biology test beckoned.

Mr Hope folded up his newspaper with a sigh. 'Yup, I'd better get going too. I've got to inspect a consignment of beef cattle arriving at Walton market.'

'Time for me to go too.' Mandy gave Jess a last hug. She hated leaving the little terrier shut up in the kitchen while she was at school. If Mandy had her way she would have tucked Jess

into her schoolbag and carted her off to lessons.
She grabbed her schoolbag. 'I expect James
is waiting.'

'No racing to school on that bike of yours,' Mr
Hope warned.

'I won't, Dad . . . 'bye, Jess,' Mandy said. 'See
you later.'

'And don't slam the door as you go out,' Mr
Hope shouted from the sink.

The front door banged loudly as Mandy
went out.

The following Monday morning there was a ring
at the back door.

'I'll go,' Mandy called from the front room
where she had been playing with Jess.

The terrier was ahead of her, hurtling down the
corridor like a bullet.

'If it's anyone for me . . .' Mr Hope dodged
away from the speeding terrier. He donned his
green waxed jacket and tweed cap. '. . . I'm off to
Baildon Farm. One of Jack Mabson's cows has got
mastitis. I should be back in about an hour.'

'Poor thing,' Mandy muttered. She knew the
inflammation of a cow's udder was terribly painful.

'You'd better hurry up then, Dad.'

Mr Hope was checking his bag. 'If it's anyone wanting anything urgent Mum can go after surgery. Or better still, get them to make an appointment with Jean.'

'Yes, Dad.' Mandy almost pushed her father out of the front door. The sooner he got to Baildon and treated that poor cow, the happier Mandy would be.

By now, Jess was hurling herself at the back door with the ferocity of a tiger, and barking furiously. Mandy ran to grab her collar. 'Jess, for goodness' sake, we're not being invaded by aliens.' Mandy scooped the noisy little dog up in her arms.

The antics of the Jack Russell always amused her. She would miss Jess so much when Aunt Mary came back. Mandy had three pet rabbits and she loved them dearly. But they weren't quite as much fun as the little terrier.

Mandy's best friend, James Hunter, stood on the doorstep.

'Oh . . . hi, James.'

James looked cold. The wind ruffled his straight brown hair. Mandy thought he looked a bit like a

Shetland pony but didn't say. She knew James was a bit sensitive and she wouldn't have hurt his feelings for all the world.

Blackie, the Hunters' black Labrador, sat at James's feet. As soon as he saw Jess, Blackie wagged his tail like mad. Jess barked and wriggled furiously. Mandy put her down. The two dogs tore off round the garden, jumping and barking.

Mandy winced. Her dad wouldn't be at all pleased if they crashed through the flower-beds. The two dogs had been great friends from the first moment Jess had come to stay at Animal Ark.

'Blackie!' James called. 'Come here!' The Labrador ignored him, belting round the garden after the agile terrier. James sighed. 'That dog never listens. *Blackie!*' Blackie gave one last excited bark and ran to sit at James's feet. He looked up at James as if to say 'sorry'.

James adjusted his glasses on the bridge of his nose. 'I thought you might want to go for a walk, Mandy,' he said.

'Oh, James, I'm sorry,' said Mandy. 'I'm going out with Mum when surgery's finished.'

James raised his eyebrows. 'Anywhere nice?'

'To Bleakfell Hall. Remember, I told you last

Friday, James. The film.'

James clapped his hand to his forehead. 'Of course you did . . . how stupid. Sorry, Mandy, I forgot.'

'We'll be back later. I'll give you a ring. We could go out then.'

'OK,' James said. 'Come on, Blackie. We'll have to go on our own this morning.' He made a face. 'Looks like I'll have to do that shopping for Mum after all.'

Mandy smiled. She knew James hated going shopping. He would rather be playing with his computer or helping Mandy at Animal Ark.

'If we have to go to Bleakfell Hall again, James, I'll ask Mum if you could come if you like.'

James grinned. 'That would be great. I'd love to.' He waved. 'See you later, Mandy.'

Jess was digging a hole in the flower-bed. Blackie had run off and stood watching.

Mandy whistled. 'Jess, Dad'll go bonkers if you dig up any more of his plants!'

James waved again as he clipped on Blackie's lead and headed off towards the village green.

Mandy felt a bit guilty. James had looked a little downhearted. She sighed. She'd buy him an ice cream later to make up for it. And, with a bit of luck, next time they had to go, James could come too.

Half an hour later Mrs Hope's four-wheel drive vehicle wound its way up the narrow road to Bleakfell Hall. The sun was warm on the windscreen. Crossing the river bridge, Mandy could see its rays hitting the water in a shower of silver sparks. She stared out of the window. The jigsaw pattern of green fields and dry-stone walls flashed past. Mandy opened the window and took a deep breath of fresh moorland air. Her heart drummed with excitement. Visiting film stars was

definitely a great way to spend the first day of the half-term!

They turned a corner and the hundred-year-old Bleakfell Hall loomed at the end of its long gravel drive. Its towers and turrets really did look like something out of a murder mystery story.

'I said it looked spooky.' Mandy peered up at the grey-stone house.

Several cars and two huge trailers were parked by the stable block. One of the trailers had 'Curtis-Smith Films Limited' written on the side in black letters.

They drew up outside the dark oak-panelled front door.

'Doesn't Mrs Ponsonby live here any more?' Mandy asked. Mrs Ponsonby was one of the bossiest women in town, and definitely a force to be reckoned with.

'Yes, I saw her in the post office on Saturday morning,' Mandy's mum confirmed. 'But she's gone to stay with her sister while they're using the house. The film company pay loads of money apparently.'

Mandy's eyes lit up. 'Hey,' she said thoughtfully. 'How about offering them an old stone cottage with a vet's surgery attached? Then we could get lots of money too!'

'Mandy!' Her mother laughed. 'You should be ashamed.'

'Not at all,' Mandy said. 'We could give it to the animal sanctuary.' Mandy's heart lurched with pity when she thought about all the wretched and abandoned animals the sanctuary took in.

Mrs Hope smiled at her daughter. 'Mrs Ponsonby really needs the money too. Some of the old house is almost falling down apparently.'

'Oh. I hope it doesn't collapse while they're filming.' Mandy took a wary look at the massive chimneys.

'I wouldn't think so, Mandy. Come on. We'd better find out who's in charge.'

'It'll be great having film stars staying near the village,' Mandy said as she got out. 'I might get their autographs. The girls at school would be really envious.' She looked round. 'I wonder where the animals are?'

'Let's find out.' Mrs Hope took her vet's bag from the car.

They went up the flight of elegant stone steps that led to the front door. Mrs Hope pressed the old-fashioned bell push.

Mandy's heart thudded with excitement as she heard light footsteps coming towards the door. It swung open. A blonde-haired young man in jeans and a college sweatshirt stood in the doorway. He held a clipboard in his hand.

'Good morning,' said Mrs Hope. 'I'm Emily Hope, the vet. I've been asked to take a look at the animals. I hope it's convenient.'

The young man grinned. Behind him, Mandy could see three or four people with ladders. They seemed to be setting up huge lights in the hallway.

'Hi,' the young man said. 'I'm Ben Burton, Mr Curtis's personal assistant. Mr Curtis is the film's director.'

'This is my daughter, Mandy.'

Mandy smiled, feeling shy. It wasn't every day she got to meet a film director's assistant!

'You'll find Mr Baggins and the others in the back kitchen,' Ben explained, stepping back for them to enter.

Mandy gulped. 'Mr Baggins. Who's he?'

Ben's eyes twinkled. 'You'd better go and see.'

Inside, the house seemed to echo with

hammering and banging. From the top of the wide, winding staircase Mandy heard a woman shouting something. The whole place was buzzing.

Suddenly a head appeared over the first floor banister. 'Ben, Mr Curtis wants you – *now*!' a young woman with a white scarf tied round her head and red dangly earrings shouted down.

'Oh, dear.' Ben looked slightly flustered. 'He'll go spare if I don't go at once. Go through into the kitchen, Mrs Hope, Mandy. Someone there will help you.' He ran his hand through his hair. 'To be honest, I'm not sure about anything at the moment. Must go!' He ran up the staircase two steps at a time.

'But . . .' Mrs Hope looked at her daughter and shrugged. 'Oh, well,' she said. 'Let's see if we can find the kitchen and Mr Baggins, whoever he might be!'

'Perhaps he's the man in charge of the animals. Funny name though,' Mandy added.

Crossing the hall seemed a bit dangerous. There were thick cables absolutely everywhere on the floor. Ladders trembled overhead. Workmen with hammers in their belts scurried around like ants.

'It's like that assault course at the adventure centre,' Mandy remarked, hopping over a thick cable that snaked across the floor.

'I think this is it.' Mrs Hope pushed open a large oak door. 'I've been here once before when Mrs Ponsonby's Pekinese was sick.'

The door led them through into a dark, oak-panelled corridor. Another door at the end was ajar. From inside a voice screeched.

'She loves you yeah, yeah, yeah! She loves you yeah, yeah, yeah! A cup of tea with two sugars, cup of tea with two sugars!'

Mandy's mum turned to look at her. They both giggled.

'I bet I know who that is!' Mandy skipped on ahead. She couldn't wait to see the owner of that strange voice.

Two

Mandy pushed open the door. She had guessed the voice came from a parrot. And there it was, sitting on the edge of the table in the huge Victorian kitchen. Beady, black eyes stared at her.

'Oh!' Mandy breathed. 'Mum, he's gorgeous!'

She stepped forward and stretched out her hand to stroke the bright red and green feathers.

'This has got to be Mr Baggins,' Mandy said. The bird arched its neck in response to Mandy's gentle caress.

'*Two cups of tea and a sugar*,' it murmured in a funny, soft voice. Mandy loved the feel of his feathers against her fingertips. Scratchy, yet soft at the same time.

'Who's a lovely boy, then?' she said softly.

A *thump, thump* came from over by the fire. Curled up on the seat was a beautiful black Labrador. Its long, silky tail beat a welcome to Mandy and Mrs Hope.

'Hello, old girl.' Mrs Hope crouched down to stroke the dog. 'Her name's Charley,' she said, examining the disc on the dog's red collar.

'She's beautiful,' Mandy said, stroking behind Charley's ears. 'I bet she's the star of the film.'

There was more. Three sleek cats were curled on the fireside rug. One purred gently, its pink nose turned upwards. All had soft, red collars with silver discs.

'This one's Snowy . . .' Mandy looked at the disc, '. . . and this one's Echo. What lovely names.' Echo, a small tabby cat, stirred and stretched lazily under Mandy's loving fingers.

'What's the grey one called?' Mrs Hope asked.

'Sky. These must be the "others" Ben told us about.'

'I guess so.' Mrs Hope looked round. 'I wonder who's in charge of them.'

Just then a tall, burly man came in through the back door. He wiped his boots on the mat. Mandy heard him sniff, then snort. He was wearing a green quilted jacket and a flat cap. His ears stuck out like jug handles and he had a rough, red face.

Charley jumped off the chair. She eyed the man suspiciously and sat down on the floor beside Mandy, pressing herself against Mandy's legs. Mandy had a strange feeling. It was as if Charley had suddenly decided Mandy was her owner – as if she wanted Mandy to look after and protect her. Mandy put her hand down and let it rest softly on Charley's sleek head. A small whine came from the Labrador's throat.

'It's OK, Charley,' Mandy whispered. 'I'll look after you, don't worry. There's no need to be nervous.' But it was clear at once to Mandy that Charley wasn't at all fond of the man who had just come into the kitchen.

'Good morning,' the man said in a deep, gravelly voice.

'Good morning.' Mrs Hope held out her hand.

'I'm Emily Hope, the vet. This is my daughter, Mandy.'

The man shook Mrs Hope's hand and nodded to Mandy. 'George Sims,' he said gruffly.

'Perhaps you can help, George,' Mrs Hope went on. 'We're looking for the person in charge of these animals.'

Mr Sims tipped his cap to the back of his head. 'It looks like I am,' he muttered.

Mrs Hope frowned. 'I don't understand.'

He pulled out a chair and sat down. Charley was still sitting against Mandy's legs. She felt the dog jump nervously at the sound of the chair legs scraping on the flagstone floor.

'There's been a bit of a problem,' Mr Sims explained. 'I do work for Animal Stars but I'm really only the driver. The girl who's supposed to supervise the animals hasn't turned up.'

'What's happened to her?' Mrs Hope asked.

Mr Sims shrugged. 'Not really sure – some mix-up about locations. She's gone off to France to do a commercial for pet food when she should be here with this lot.'

'Oh, dear,' said Mrs Hope.

'They've asked me to stay until she turns up,'

Mr Sims went on grumpily. 'I mean what do I know about looking after a parrot?'

Mr Baggins squawked, '*Mr Sugar, cup of bags.*'

Mandy giggled, then put her hand over her mouth.

'Well,' Mrs Hope said, 'I'm sure we could give you any advice you need. Especially if its only for a day or so. I'm sure the agency will send someone as soon as possible.'

'I jolly well hope so,' Mr Sims said, still looking grumpy.

Snowy, the white cat, got up from his place by the fire. Purring, he rubbed himself against Mr Sims's corduroy trousers, arching his back and waving his tail like a flag.

Mr Sims moved his legs away. Mandy stepped forward and picked Snowy up, cradling him in her arms.

'Can't stand cats,' George Sims muttered. He glared at Mr Baggins. 'Nor parrots.'

Mr Baggins stared back at him with beady eyes.

'*Left, right, left, right, quick march!*' Mr Baggins suddenly screeched.

Mandy put her hand over her mouth to stop

herself from bursting into laughter.

'Bah!' said Mr Sims.

Mandy bit her lip, suddenly feeling serious. How on earth could anyone dislike either Snowy or Mr Baggins? Both of them were beautiful and perfectly harmless.

'Right,' Mrs Hope went on in a businesslike way. 'My job is to examine the animals. Shall I do it here?'

George Sims shrugged. 'If you like.'

Charley suddenly got up and ran through a door beside the old pine dresser.

'Charley!' Mandy called. 'Where's she going?' she asked Mr Sims.

'She's made her bed in the pantry,' Mr Sims said. 'Best place for her. Keeps her out of the way until she's needed.'

Mandy felt sorry for the Labrador, hiding away in a cold pantry when a cosy fire burned in the hearth.

'Who shall I give the certificate to?' Mrs Hope was asking.

'Certificate?' Mr Sims looked blank.

'Yes, I have to pass the animals as fit before the film company can use them.'

'Leave it on the table if you like. I'll pick it up after my break.'

Mandy was trying to persuade Charley to come out of the pantry.

'Come on, Charley. Mum wants to have a look at you.'

'I should leave her,' Mr Sims said, opening the back door. 'She's a bit moody if you ask me.'

'Well, she is an actor,' Mandy said. She thought George Sims might feel moody too if he was being looked after by someone who didn't much like him.

Mr Sims snorted. He went out and slammed the door behind him.

'He's not very keen on animals, is he, Mum?' Mandy said. She coaxed the Labrador out of the pantry. 'Come on, Charley, Mum won't hurt you.'

'I think he's just a bit worried,' Mrs Hope replied. 'He's had the job rather thrust upon him by the looks of it. Let's hope the proper trainer arrives soon.'

Mandy sat on the floor with her arms round the Labrador's neck. She rubbed her cheek against the shining coat. Her heart stirred. If George Sims just took time to get to know Charley he'd

soon find out how gorgeous she was.

'Come on, Charley.' Mrs Hope lifted the big dog on to the table. 'Let's have a look at you then.'

She examined the dog gently. Ears . . . eyes . . . teeth. All looked fine. She felt Charley's sleek, muscled back and ran her hands over her legs. She held Charley's head between her hands and looked at her muzzle. Then she ruffled the hair on the back of Charley's head and lifted her down.

'She's great,' Mrs Hope said. 'A picture of health.'

'Are you going to look at Mr Baggins?' Mandy asked when her mum had finished examining the three cats.

'*Mr Baggins . . . Mr Baggins!*' the parrot suddenly screeched. '*A cup of tea and two Baggins.*'

Mandy burst out laughing. Mrs Hope laughed too. 'Yes, but I'm almost certain there's nothing wrong with him,' she said.

Mrs Hope carefully wrapped the bird in a tea towel and gently examined him. She stroked the parrot's feathers and put him back on the table. 'His claws look a bit long but nothing to worry about.'

Suddenly Mr Baggins took off, flying up and landing on one of the high oak beams of the ceiling.

'I wonder what part he plays in the film?' Mandy asked.

'A naughty part, I should think.' Mrs Hope took a book from her bag. She sat at the table and wrote something on one of the pages. 'I think I'd better wait to explain these certificates to George.'

'Do you think it's OK if I take a look round the house?' Mandy asked. 'I'd love to see the film set.'

'I should think so. Don't get in anyone's way, though. It looked pretty chaotic out there.'

'I'll take Charley,' Mandy spied a dog lead hanging from a hook on the back door.

'And don't be too long,' Mrs Hope added. 'I've got to call on Mrs Platt on the way back.'

Mandy's heart skipped a beat. She knew Mrs Platt's poodle had been ill for a long time. 'Not Brandy again?' she said anxiously.

Mrs Hope looked grim. 'Yes, I'm afraid so. Mrs Platt rang this morning and asked me to call in to look at him.'

'Oh, dear.' Mandy's heart sank. Brandy, Mrs Platt's poodle, was very old and had trouble with his kidneys. Mandy had a horrible feeling that this time there wouldn't be any pills that would make him better.

Mrs Hope patted Mandy's arm. 'Cheer up, Mandy. It may not be as bad as you think.'

'I hope not,' Mandy said. 'I don't know what Mrs Platt will do without a dog. She'll be really lonely.'

Mrs Platt's husband had died over a year ago. Since then, Brandy had been her only companion.

She had a son but he lived miles away in London and couldn't visit very often.

Mandy pulled herself together. There was no use worrying about it. Whatever happened, neither Mrs Platt nor her mum would want poor Brandy to suffer.

'Come on, Charley,' she said. 'Let's see if we can spot any film stars out there.'

In the hall, a single huge spotlight was being erected in the corner. A short, balding man with an extremely large stomach and a loud voice to match was shouting instructions. He wore an out-of-shape grey T-shirt that announced he was 'The Boss'.

'No – point it this way!' he yelled. 'We want it to look as if the light's coming through the window, not from a hole in the ceiling!'

'Hello, young lady.' The man had spotted Mandy. 'Are you the animal trainer?'

'Er – no,' Mandy stammered. 'I'm Mandy Hope, the vet's daughter. I'm just taking Charley for a little look round.'

The man bent down to pat Charley affectionately. Mandy could see he liked dogs. She always knew when people were good with animals. And, as far as Mandy was concerned, anyone who liked animals had got to be a nice person.

'Is Charley the star?' Mandy asked.

'She surely is.' The man looked over his shoulder. 'But don't tell Antonia that.'

'Antonia?'

'Miss Antonia Kent. Our *human* star.'

Mandy giggled.

'The dog sees it all happen.'

'Gosh!' Mandy's eyes were wide. 'Sees what . . . not the murder?'

The man looked sombre. 'Yes, the dirty deed itself. The lady of the manor stabs her husband in a fit of jealousy in this very hallway. Her pet dog – she's called Black Rose in the story – witnesses the terrible crime.'

Mandy was staring at him, wide-eyed. 'Wow!' She felt quite breathless.

'Why don't you stay to watch the filming?' the man said. 'Maybe Charley will give a truly great performance if you're here. You two certainly look as if you're great friends already.'

'We are.' Mandy grinned. She felt pleased the man had noticed how well she and Charley were getting along. She patted Charley's head affectionately. 'I'd love to stay and watch.' Then she remembered something important she had to do. Her face fell. 'Oh . . . but I can't. I'm sorry. I've got to go back with my mum.'

Mandy would love to have stayed with Charley. But she had to see Mrs Platt's dear little Brandy. And if he was so ill that nothing could be done to cure him then Mrs Platt might well need a shoulder to cry on.

Just then, Ben came running down the stairs.

'There you are, Mr Curtis!'

'Mr Curtis!' Mandy gasped. She hadn't realised the man really was 'The Boss'!

'I've been looking all over for you,' Ben went on. 'Miss Kent's throwing a tantrum again.'

The sound of crashing china came from one of the upstairs rooms. *Oh dear*, Mandy thought. *That's not all she's throwing.*

Mr Curtis sighed heavily. 'What now, Ben?'

'She says she won't work with a parrot. She says she's allergic to birds and that it might have fleas or something.'

'Fleas!' Mandy couldn't help blurting out. 'Mr Baggins has got nothing of the sort.'

Mr Curtis sighed again. He turned to Mandy. 'These actresses are so temperamental. I'd better go and calm her down. Ben, look after this young lady, will you?'

Just then, Mrs Hope came through from the kitchen. Charley wagged her tail in greeting.

'Mum,' Mandy said. 'This is Mr Curtis, the film's director.'

Mrs Hope shook his hand. 'The animals are all fine,' she said. 'You can begin using them whenever you're ready.' She handed him the certificate. 'I was going to give this to George Sims but I can't wait any longer.'

Mandy saw Ben and Mr Curtis exchange worried glances.

'I'm afraid he's not turning out to be very reliable,' Ben said with a frown. 'Let's hope the proper trainer turns up soon.'

'Yes,' Mrs Hope agreed. 'Let's hope so.'

Mr Curtis strode off up the stairs.

Ben took Charley's lead from Mandy's hand and ushered them to the front door.

'Could I bring my friend James next time?' asked Mandy. 'He's mad about animals.'

'I don't see why not,' Ben replied. 'And as

George doesn't seem to have much idea what to do with them, it looks as if we might be very glad of your help!'

Three

'I'm a bit worried about Charley,' Mandy said as they drove back down into Welford. They went along the upper high street, past the church, past the Old School House adult education centre that used to be the village school until a few years ago. They soon reached the estate of modern bungalows where Mrs Platt lived with Brandy.

'Why?' Mandy's mother glanced in her direction.

'She just doesn't seem very happy.' Mandy had

been worrying about Charley ever since they left the hall. 'A dog needs love and affection, not a smelly old blanket on the floor of a cold pantry.'

Mrs Hope patted her daughter's knee. 'She's OK, Mandy. She's just taking a little time to settle down. Remember how Jess was when she first came to stay with us?'

Mandy managed a small smile. 'Yes,' she said. 'I think she missed her boyfriend.'

'Who, Tad?' Tad was the Jack Russell that lived next door to Aunt Mary. Mrs Hope laughed. 'Yes, I expect you're right, Mandy. And don't worry about Charley. We'll keep a good eye on her.'

Mandy felt reassured. Her mother was always right.

They drew up outside a semi-detached bungalow with a large back garden at the end of the row. They got out and went round past rows of neatly planted vegetables to the back door.

Mrs Platt hurried to answer their knock.

'Thank goodness you're here,' she said anxiously. 'I was afraid I'd missed you. I just had to pop along to the church to renew the water in the vases.' Mrs Platt was well known in the village for her floral arrangements. 'Come in, come in.'

The bungalow kitchen was warm and cosy. Pots and pans shone on the shelves and bright red and blue curtains adorned the windows.

'I've kept the radiator on for poor Brandy,' Mrs Platt explained. 'I thought he might feel better if he was tucked up nice and warm.' Her voice trembled a little. Mandy felt really sorry for Mrs Platt.

Brandy, a miniature champagne poodle, lay in his basket. Mandy felt her throat swell and her eyes began to fill with tears. The little dog's eyes were red and weepy, and his coat looked dull. 'Poor Brandy,' she whispered. She remembered Brandy when he was bright and active, a dear, friendly little animal. She crouched down beside the basket.

Mrs Hope gently probed the dog's swollen stomach. Her fingers touched a tender spot and the poodle gave a little whine. Mandy winced. She wished she could take the dog's pain away.

Mrs Hope rose. Her face looked sad. 'I'm sorry, Mrs Platt. If those tablets I gave him last week haven't worked . . .'

Mrs Platt shook her head. 'He did seem a bit

better. We even went for a little walk yesterday
when I got in from church. But this morning he
wouldn't even get out of his basket. I had to carry
him out to do his business.'

Mandy stroked Brandy's curly coat. The little
dog felt hot, and his nose was dry. She felt a tear
creep from beneath her eyelid and trickle down
her cheek. It fell on Brandy's fur.

'He's in a good deal of pain, I'm afraid,' Mrs
Hope was saying. 'I really think the kindest thing
would be to put him to sleep.'

Mandy looked up through a mist of tears. Mrs
Hope had her arm round Mrs Platt's shoulders.

'Yes,' Mrs Platt nodded. 'You're right, of course.
We can't let him suffer. If you're absolutely
sure . . . ?'

Mrs Hope nodded sadly. 'I can give him an
injection now, or you could bring him along to
the surgery.'

'No . . . no.' Mrs Platt took a hanky from her
trouser pocket and blew her nose loudly. 'Brandy
would want to go to sleep in his own basket.'

Mrs Hope opened her bag and took out a
syringe.

Mandy wiped her eyes with the back of her

hand. She drew in a deep breath. It really was no good crying. All the tears in the world wouldn't make Brandy better. She tried to pull herself together. 'Would you like me to help you, Mum?'

'No, it's all right, thanks. Why don't you take Mrs Platt into the garden? Take a look at those lovely roses. Unless you want to stay?'

Mrs Platt shook her head. 'No. I'm not very good at this sort of thing.' She knelt down by Brandy's basket. The little dog lifted his head at the sight of his mistress. Mrs Platt stroked his head gently. Mandy could see she was crying.

Mrs Platt bent and touched Brandy's head with her lips. Mandy put a hand out to steady her as she rose to her feet.

'Come on, Mrs Platt. Let's see those roses.'

Mandy shut the door gently behind them. She swallowed the tears that threatened to spill over once again. There seemed to be a hard lump in her throat.

She linked her arm through Mrs Platt's as they walked slowly up the garden path. Mrs Platt blew her nose once then seemed to recover.

'There's no use crying,' she said in a determined voice. 'Brandy has had a wonderful life. He's

been treated like a little prince. It's wrong to let him suffer.'

Mandy managed a sad little smile. 'Yes.' Mrs Platt was right, of course, but it was still horrible to think they would never see Brandy alive again.

'See this . . .' Mrs Platt pointed to a pink climbing rose just coming into flower. 'I brought this with me from my old house. My husband gave it to me for my birthday – the same birthday my son gave Brandy to me.' She sighed. 'What a gorgeous little puppy Brandy was. Nothing but a bundle of fluff with two huge black eyes—'

Her voice broke. 'He's twelve years old you know, Mandy.'

'Same age as me,' Mandy said softly. They looked at each other and smiled. There was a bond of understanding between them. Dear little Brandy wouldn't be running up the garden any more but at least Mrs Platt had this beautiful rose to remember him by.

'Will you get another dog?' Mandy asked as they reached the end of the garden and looked out towards the high moors. She felt a bit better. It was time to think about the future and not the past.

Mrs Platt shook her head. 'I'm afraid I can't afford one. I don't earn much with my little job at the grocer's shop.'

Mandy turned to see her mother standing by the back door drying her hands on a towel. They walked back towards her.

'How . . . ?' Mrs Platt began. Mandy heard a tremble in her voice.

'He just went to sleep peacefully,' Mrs Hope assured her.

Mandy squeezed Mrs Platt's arm.

'What would you like me to do with Brandy,

now, Mrs Platt?' Mrs Hope asked gently. 'I've wrapped him in his blanket.'

Mandy looked past her mum and Mrs Platt. She could just see a pathetic little bundle wrapped in a blue blanket lying in Brandy's basket. She felt the tears coming again but managed to hold them back.

'I'll see to him, don't worry,' replied Mrs Platt. 'I'll bury him beneath the rose. 'He'll like it there. It was his favourite place on a hot summer's day. Nice and shady, you see.'

Mandy could just imagine Brandy as he used to be, and she knew they had done the right thing.

'How much do I owe you, Emily?' Mrs Platt said in a practical voice. She squared her shoulders. Mandy admired her bravery. She didn't think she would ever get used to animals having to die this way.

'Don't worry about that. I'll get Jean to send the bill at the end of the month.'

Mandy gave Mrs Platt a hug. 'I hope you won't be too lonely.'

Mrs Platt managed a wan smile. 'Maybe I'll get a budgie. They're not so expensive to keep.'

'No, but you can't take a budgie for a walk,' Mandy said sadly.

Mrs Platt watched from the window as they drove away. Mandy thought she looked so lonely with no little dog to cuddle in her arms.

They headed straight back to Animal Ark. The village high street was quiet.

Mrs Hope patted her daughter's knee. 'Cheer up, Mandy.'

'I'm trying to,' Mandy said. 'I just know how Mrs Platt will miss poor Brandy.'

'I know, darling.'

Mandy looked thoughtful. 'You know, Mum, Mrs Platt would really love another poodle. She just can't afford one.'

'They are pretty expensive.' Mrs Hope changed gear to go round the sharp bend.

'I know. That's what she said. I've been thinking . . .'

'What?' Mrs Hope glanced knowingly at her daughter. 'What scheme are you cooking up now, Mandy?'

'I just thought maybe they'd have one at the animal sanctuary.'

'Yes, they might.' Mrs Hope raised her eyebrows.

Mandy jiggled about in her seat. 'Could we go up there now?'

'Hang on a minute, Mandy. Give Mrs Platt time to get over poor old Brandy.'

'But having a new pet will help her,' Mandy insisted. Once Mandy had an idea in her head, wild horses wouldn't drag it away.

'We'll go as soon as your dad or I have a spare minute. Does that suit you?'

Mandy sighed. 'Yes, OK, but you won't forget, will you?'

'I don't suppose you'll let me!'

They pulled up under the wooden sign that said 'Animal Ark, Veterinary Surgeon'.

Mandy jumped out, anxious to see Jess. She felt better now. The thought of finding a new dog for Mrs Platt had cheered her up no end.

'I'll just check with Jean to see if there's been any calls.' Mrs Hope headed for the surgery door.

Mandy hurried through into the kitchen. Jess was curled up in her basket, fast asleep. She hadn't even heard the door open.

'Jess!'

The little dog opened her eyes sleepily as Mandy bent to cuddle her.

'Jess,' Mandy said again. 'You lazy old thing. You didn't even hear me come in. You're getting to be a real lazybones.'

Jess licked her face. Mandy picked her up and gave her a quick cuddle.

Mandy went to the phone and dialled James's number. He answered after a dozen rings.

'Oh . . .' Mandy said. 'I was just about to give up.'

'Sorry,' James said. 'I was playing with my new computer game.'

Mandy screwed up her nose. She hated computer games. 'Do you still want to come over later?' she asked.

'You bet. How did you get on at Bleakfell Hall?'

'It was great. I'll tell you all about it when you get here.'

After lunch, Mandy helped Simon, Animal Ark's nurse, with his jobs at the back of the surgery. Simon was laying newspapers on the bottom of one of the animal cages. Mandy was washing and drying the feed bowls.

'Simon?' Mandy said. 'Any idea if the animal

sanctuary would have a poodle for Mrs Platt?'

Simon, a young man in his twenties, tall and thin with fair hair, shrugged his shoulders. 'I don't know, Mandy. I know they get all sorts of dogs handed in.'

Mandy breathed a sigh. 'Aren't people horrible?' she said, suddenly feeling angry as she always did at the thought of all the abandoned and unwanted animals at the sanctuary.

Simon gave a little smile. '*Some* people are, Mandy. Not everyone.'

'You know what I mean.' Mandy thought of Simon as a good friend. Someone to talk things over with if her mum and dad were a bit too busy to listen straight away.

'I mean people who abandon animals,' Mandy went on, still feeling angry. 'Remember that cat I found? Walton. We thought someone had abandoned her because she was pregnant. I was so angry. Why don't people realise a pet is for life, not something you can throw away like . . . like . . .' Mandy felt so indignant all of a sudden she couldn't think of the right word.

'Like an empty cornflake box?' Simon suggested.

'Exactly,' Mandy said.

'You know it's not always people's own fault.' Simon tried to calm her down. 'Sometimes people move house and can't take their pet . . . sometimes they just can't cope with them any longer.'

'Yes, I suppose so,' Mandy agreed. 'But people *should* be more responsible.'

'Can't argue with that,' Simon said with a grin.

Mandy stacked the feed bowls inside one another and put the damp tea towel in the dirty linen basket. She looked at her watch. 'Is there anything else I can do to help, Simon? James should be here in a minute. We're taking the dogs for a walk.'

'No, thanks, Mandy.' Simon was washing his hands. 'That's great.'

Just then James arrived. He handed Mandy a packet of sherbet. 'I got you this at the shop,' he said, grinning. 'I know it's your favourite.'

Mandy was going to hug him then thought he might be embarrassed in front of Simon. 'Thanks, James,' she said. 'Come on. I'll tell you all about Charley, the film star dog.'

Four

The next morning Mandy jumped out of bed. The garden sparkled in the morning sun. There had been a storm in the night. Mandy had woken once to a tremendous crack of thunder.

She had a tight knot of excitement in her stomach. With a bit of luck George Sims would ring from Bleakfell Hall today to say the horses had arrived. She would get to see Charley and Mr Baggins again!

But when the telephone rang it was Grandad.

'Will you be coming to see us during the holiday, Mandy?' he asked as she picked up the receiver.

Mandy smiled. She loved visiting her grandparents at Lilac Cottage, just up the lane from Animal Ark.

'Yes, 'course, Grandad. I'm hoping to go out with Mum this morning, but James and I could come over later if you like.'

'Oh, good. Your Gran's trying out this new recipe for chocolate orange cake and she thought you might like to try it,' Grandad said.

'Yum,' said Mandy. 'We'll definitely be over later, Grandad.'

Mandy felt a bit restless. She'd got her chores to do in the surgery but couldn't seem to settle down to anything. Luckily, the call from Bleakfell Hall came just a few minutes later.

'The horses have arrived,' Mrs Hope said, popping her head round the door.

'Great!' Mandy said excitedly, full of energy all of a sudden. 'I'll ring James.'

James arrived on his bike just as they were getting in the car. Mandy could see he had rushed. His tracksuit top was on back to front but she figured she'd wait to tell him.

Jess climbed on to James's lap, curled up and fell asleep straight away.

When they arrived at Bleakfell Hall they could hear a lot of shouting from inside.

They left Jess curled up in the back of the car, making sure to leave the windows open.

'Perhaps we'd better go round to the yard,' Mrs Hope suggested. 'It sounds as if they're pretty busy in there. I know where the stables are.'

'Let's go and find Charley,' Mandy said to James.

There was no answer to their knock on the back door. Cautiously, Mandy opened it and put her head round.

'Hello . . . anybody here?' She turned to James. 'Come on, I'm sure they won't mind if we go in.'

The vast kitchen was empty. No Charley, no Mr Baggins, no cats, no George Sims. Where on earth was everyone?

The sound of Mr Curtis's voice came echoing along the passage that led to the great hallway.

Mandy pulled James's sleeve. 'Come on, let's take a look. Perhaps all the animals are on the set.'

They crept along the corridor and peered round the half-open door.

The place was in an uproar.

Mandy stifled a giggle. 'I told you it was chaotic,' she whispered to James.

Mr Curtis sat on top of a stepladder, waving his arms about. The ladder wobbled. Ben rushed forward to steady it. Mandy put her hand over her mouth to stop the laughter coming out.

'No!' Mr Curtis was shouting. 'Not there – for goodness' sake, someone get hold of that parrot!'

A woman in an ankle-length white frock was sitting by the fireplace. There was a blanket over her head. The cats were asleep on the sofa as if nothing was going on.

'That must be Antonia Kent,' Mandy whispered in James's ear. 'She's the human star.'

'I'm not acting with that beastly bird!' a voice came from under the blanket. 'I'm not, I'm not, I'm not!'

'Look!' Mandy said, suddenly spying the parrot. 'There's Mr Baggins!'

Sure enough, high up on the elegant, crystal chandelier, Mr Baggins preened his feathers.

Beneath, an assistant held up a cup of sunflower seeds.

'Come down, Mr Baggins,' she was shouting. 'Nice dinner.'

'*Two sugars!*' the parrot screeched. '*A cup of Baggins if you please.*'

Mandy was laughing so much she felt sure someone would hear.

'Where's that blasted George Sims?' Mr Curtis yelled suddenly. 'He's supposed to be supervising these wretched creatures.'

'What a mess,' James whispered.

'We'd better get out of here before we get told off,' Mandy said.

But it was too late. They had been spotted.

'Ah, young lady,' Mr Curtis called from his ladder. 'Come in, come in. Any hope of you getting that bird to come down?'

Mandy and James sidled into the hall. Mandy looked up. 'I'll try,' she said. She felt a bit shy in front of all of the crew. 'But I can't promise.'

Across the hall, Antonia Kent peeped out from under her blanket. Mandy almost laughed again. The actress looked like a nun in a dance frock with the white blanket round her face. But when she took the blanket right off, Mandy drew in her breath. She recognised her straight away. Antonia Kent was the heroine of one of Mandy's favourite soap operas! She just couldn't help staring.

'Mandy . . .' James nudged her in the ribs.

'Oh!' Mandy shook herself. She stood under the chandelier. 'Mr Baggins,' she called softly. 'Come on down, Mr Baggins. You're being very naughty.'

'*She loves you yeah, yeah, yeah,*' Mr Baggins said.

'Yes,' Mandy couldn't help grinning. 'I know, but please come down, huh?'

Mandy heard laughter echoing round the set. She glanced at Mr Curtis. He had a face like thunder. He definitely didn't think it was funny even if everyone else did.

Mandy pursed her lips. She pretended to frown. 'Now come on, Mr Baggins, stop mucking about.' Someone passed her the bowl of sunflower seeds and she held them out. 'Come on . . . please.'

To Mandy's relief, Mr Baggins cocked his head on one side, spread his bright wings, and fluttered down towards her. He landed on her head. Mandy tottered. Then she caught sight of herself

in a big, gold framed wall mirror. She looked as
if she was wearing a gaily coloured hat in an
Easter parade. She put her hand up. 'Come on,
you rotten thing. You're holding everyone up.'

Mr Baggins stepped daintily on to her fingers.
A sigh of relief washed round the room.

'Well *done*, darling.' Antonia Kent swept towards
Mandy in a wave of pale silk and strong perfume.
She had black hair, tied up in curls on top of her
head, and a pale complexion with a dark beauty
spot on her rouged cheek. The actress eyed the
parrot warily as she put her arm round Mandy's
shoulders. 'This girl's got a magic touch.' She
turned to the crew. 'Is she the new animal trainer?
Has that hopeless man gone at last?'

Mr Curtis wobbled down his ladder. 'No,' he
said. 'She's the vet's daughter. That was terrific,
Mandy. Maybe you could stay and help out? We
need Charley next. Perhaps you'd fetch her?'

'Oh, yes,' Mandy's heart leapt with excitement.
'I'd love to.'

Just then the front door opened and George
Sims came through into the hall. He looked upset.
His green wellies were covered with mud. His
face was red, as if he had been running.

'Ah, Sims,' Mr Curtis said, 'I was just sending Mandy to fetch the dog.'

George Sims bit his lip. 'The dog's gone,' he said gruffly, looking down at the toes of his boots. 'Run off.'

'What!' Mr Curtis groaned.

Mandy's stomach turned icy with fear. 'Oh, no!' she cried. 'When?'

George Sims looked at her. His face was full of remorse. 'I put her out last night and she didn't come back in. The thunder – it must have scared her.'

A tide of anger and fear washed over Mandy. How could anyone be so daft? 'You put her out during a storm? Don't you know dogs hate thunder?' she exploded.

Mr Sims pursed his lips. 'I didn't know, did I? I told you I'm only the driver. Anyway, she seemed to have settled down. I thought she'd be OK.'

Mandy whirled round. 'Come on, James, we'd better go and look for her.'

'If the dog's been gone all night,' Ben said, 'she could be anywhere.'

'I've been out there looking.' George Sims took

off his cap and scratched his head. 'She's gone, that's for sure.'

'Well, we're going to look anyway.' Mandy's eyes blazed. She and James dashed from the hall.

'Where shall we start?' James panted behind her.

'We'll get Jess. She's good at sniffing scents.'

'But she's never met Charley.'

Mandy was already opening the tail-gate of the car. 'Come on, Jess.' She clipped on the terrier's lead. 'We'll let her sniff Charley's blanket. That might do the trick.'

They ran round the back and into the kitchen. 'Look, Jess.' Mandy thrust open the pantry door. Jess ran inside. She sniffed Charley's blanket and made a little whine in her throat. She began scratching it up to make a bed.

'No, Jess!' Mandy pulled the lead gently. 'No time to sleep now. Charley is missing and we've got to find her!'

'We'd better tell your mum,' James said.

They dashed out into the yard. In the stable, Mrs Hope was examining a beautiful bay gelding. 'What on earth's happened?' Mrs Hope asked in surprise.

'It's Charley,' Mandy blurted. 'She's run off.'

'Run off . . . oh, dear. When?'

'Last night.' Mandy's voice broke. The thought of the beautiful Labrador lost on the moors was awful.

'Mr Sims let her out during the storm,' James explained. 'She must have been really scared. He's been looking for her all morning.'

'We're taking Jess to look for her,' Mandy said.

'It might be an idea to search the outbuildings,' Mrs Hope said. 'She could be hiding.'

'Good thinking,' Mandy said. 'Come on, James. Let's go.'

'Mandy, don't go far. I've got to get back to the surgery and don't forget you promised to visit Gran and Grandad.'

'But we can't just leave . . .'

'I'm sorry, Mandy. Look, there's all the crew to look for her.' Mrs Hope put her arm round Mandy's shoulders. 'I'm sure they'll find her. Just do what you can while you're here. OK?'

Mandy sniffed, then nodded. 'OK, Mum. Come on, James. Let's go.'

* * *

By the time Mrs Hope was ready to leave, the outbuildings had been thoroughly combed for signs of the missing dog.

'Charley! Charley!' They had looked all over. The stables, the hay loft, the old dairy. Mandy and James and Jess had run round the grounds, peering in the shrubbery, the old walled kitchen garden, the tool-shed. They had even gone up into the attic of Bleakfell Hall. But Charley was nowhere to be seen. Eventually it was time to get back.

As they drove down the road, Mandy felt miserable. What had promised to be such a great day had turned out to be just rotten.

'Cheer up, Mandy.' Her mother put a reassuring hand on Mandy's knee. 'You've done all you can to find Charley. The dog is really the film company's responsibility, not ours.'

'I know,' said Mandy. 'But I *told* Charley I'd look after her. I can't let her down.'

In the back of the car James sat silently hugging the tired terrier. It seemed as if they had run for miles in their hunt for the missing dog, and they were both exhausted.

'We haven't really done *anything*,' Mandy

suddenly felt angry. She looked at her mother. 'All we've done is searched some silly old buildings and garden. Charley could be miles away by now and we're doing nothing to help.'

'You'll have to be content with that for now, Mandy,' Mrs Hope said firmly. 'We're going up to Syke Farm. I rang Jean from Bleakfell Hall to see if there were any messages. Mrs Janeki wants me to look at a ewe that's been injured. If you keep a lookout, you might see Charley.'

Mandy sighed. She gazed out of the window. She just wished they hadn't had to leave when they did.

Ahead, the moors and dales seemed to stretch endlessly into the distance. The thought of Charley out there somewhere, lonely and lost, was almost too much to bear. Charley could be lying injured at the bottom of a high rock, shivering with wet and cold . . . hungry. Mandy couldn't stop the rush of terrible thoughts.

'We could ask around the village when we get back,' James said in a small voice. 'Someone might have seen Charley.'

'Yes, you're right, James,' Mandy said, her head clearing. She realised there was lots they could do. 'We could put posters up,' she said, brightening.

'You see,' Mrs Hope said, changing gear to turn into Syke Farm. 'You've only just begun to help.'

Mandy felt a lot better as the car pulled into the farmyard. It was certainly no use moping about. You had to think positive. And thinking positive meant doing everything they could to find Charley!

In the farmyard, Mr Janeki stood in the doorway of the barn. He wore brown overalls and black, muddy wellingtons. His round face looked grim.

'Better stay in the car, you two,' Mrs Hope said, getting out. 'I shan't be long.'

Mandy saw the farmer greet Mrs Hope. They stood talking. Mr Janeki pointed his finger towards the field that bordered the farmyard. Then he and Mrs Hope disappeared into the barn.

Mandy turned to James. 'We'll tell Gran and Grandad about Charley,' she said. 'They'll have some ideas. Gran's always a help if you're in trouble. And Grandad might take us out in his camper to search the dales.'

'Great idea.' James brightened up. 'And I'll do all I can to help.'

'Thanks, James,' Mandy said with a sigh. It was great to have such a good friend, she thought.

Mrs Hope came out of the barn with Mr Janeki. Her face was grave as she came towards the car and got in.

'What's up, Mum?' Mandy asked.

'One of Mr Janeki's sheep has been attacked by a dog,' Mrs Hope said with a worried frown.

Mandy's hand flew to her mouth. 'You don't think . . .'

Her mother's face was serious. 'Yes, I'm afraid so, Mandy. It could well have been Charley!'

Five

'But how do you know it could be Charley?' Mandy insisted. 'Surely she wouldn't do a thing like that?'

'Well, it was a black dog. It could have been her,' Mrs Hope said as the four-wheel drive headed for the village and Lilac Cottage. 'And you know, Mandy, if it *was* Charley, she could be shot.'

'I know.' Mandy's heart lurched with fear. 'That's why we've got to find her, Mum,' she said determinedly. 'As soon as possible.'

As they drew up outside the house, Mandy could see her grandfather mowing the lawn beneath the huge lilac tree that gave the cottage its name. Mandy loved the smell of new-cut grass. It reminded her of summery days and Gran's homemade lemonade on the lawn.

Mandy, James and Jess climbed out of the car and went through the front gate.

'This grass seems to grow as fast as I cut it,' Grandad said stopping the mower's engine and giving Mandy a hug. 'Hiya James,' he added with a grin.

'Hello, Mr Hope,' James said cheerfully.

Grandad bent to stroke Jess. 'Hello, Jack Russell. She's getting fat, Mandy.'

'I know. Dad says I'm feeding her too much, but she always seems to be hungry.'

Grandad waved goodbye to Mrs Hope as she drew away from the kerb. 'Come on, you two. Let's go and find your gran. The smell of that chocolate cake's been driving me mad all morning.' He ushered them past his bicycle leaning up against the wall, past the fragrant herb garden and into the warm and cosy cottage kitchen. 'The camper's in for a service,' he explained, 'so I've been using my bike to go into Walton.

'They're here, Dorothy!' Grandad called. Mandy could hear the sound of music and someone giving some kind of instructions. 'She's doing her aerobics,' Grandad said with a wink. 'Dorothy!' He disappeared into the back room. Mandy heard the video recorder being switched off. A moment later Gran appeared in her green tracksuit, looking red in the face.

She gave Mandy a hug. 'Mandy! It's great to see you. And you, James. Now, how about a slice of cake?'

She went to the pantry and brought out a huge chocolate cake with orange icing on the top. Mandy saw James's eyes open wide in amazement. 'Fancy some milk as well?' asked Gran.

'Yes, please,' they chorused. Mandy tried her best to look cheerful but she saw her grandmother glance knowingly at her worried face.

'What's up, Mandy?' Gran cut four slices of cake and put them on pretty porcelain plates. 'Tell us what's wrong.'

Suddenly it all poured out: the visit to Bleakfell

Hall; how George Sims had let poor Charley out in the thunderstorm; how she had gone missing; how they had searched in vain.

'And Mr Janeki's sheep have been attacked,' Mandy added, close to tears. 'We're really scared it might be Charley, aren't we, James?'

James nodded, his mouth full of cake.

'. . . and now we're going to ask round the village and make some posters saying Charley's missing,' Mandy added. 'Can you think of anything else we can do, Gran?'

'I'd have taken you out in the camper to look for her if it was here,' Grandad said.

'Never mind, Grandad,' Mandy said with a sigh. 'It can't be helped.'

Mandy's grandmother looked thoughtful. 'You know they have a programme on local radio where you can phone in. Maybe you could do that, Mandy – put out a message about Charley?' She rose and went to the sideboard. 'I've got their number written down in my telephone book.'

Grandad rose and wiped his mouth. 'That was really yummy, Dorothy. Oh, well, better finish that lawn before it rains.'

Mandy took Gran's telephone book and went

into the back room where the phone was. She dialled quickly. She felt a bit nervous. She had never spoken to anyone at a radio station before.

'Radio Yorkshire.' They answered straight away.

'Umm . . .' Mandy said. 'Could you put me through to the afternoon show, please.'

There were several clicks, then a man's voice answered. 'Yes. Can I help you?'

Mandy quickly explained about Charley. '. . . so if anyone sees a black Labrador with a red collar would they please ring Welford 703627.' Mandy felt quite breathless after rushing to tell the story.

'Yes, we'll put that out about three o'clock,' the man said.

'Oh, thank you,' Mandy breathed.

'Good luck,' the man said. Mandy heard another click as he put the phone down.

She went back into the kitchen. 'They're putting out a call on the afternoon show,' she said. 'That should help, shouldn't it?' She ran to hug her grandmother. 'Thanks, Gran, you're brilliant. Come on, James, let's go and ask if anyone's seen Charley round the village!'

Mandy's grandparents stood at the gate to wave goodbye.

'Where shall we go first?' James said, racing to keep up.

'We'll try the post office,' Mandy said.

The village post office sold more than just stamps. In fact it sold just about everything. Newspapers, groceries, pegs, sweets, even paper-clips.

The small bell clanged as Mandy went in. James stayed outside with Jess as dogs weren't allowed in the shop.

The postmistress, Mrs McFarlane, was behind the counter.

'Hello, Mandy.'

'Mrs McFarlane,' Mandy said. 'Have you seen a black Labrador dog at all?'

'You mean Blackie, James Hunter's dog? Has he got lost?'

Mandy shook her head. 'No . . . like Blackie, but a female dog. She's with the film company up at Bleakfell Hall but she's gone missing.'

Mrs McFarlane shook her head. She was a kindly lady and she knew everyone's business. If anyone had seen Charley, Mrs McFarlane would know. 'No, I'm sorry, Mandy, I haven't.'

'If we do a poster about her, would you put it in the window?'

Mrs McFarlane smiled. 'Of course, Mandy. I'd be glad to.'

'Thanks, Mrs McFarlane.' Mandy felt pleased. It was great to live in a place like Welford where everyone was willing to help out.

Outside, James waited. 'Any luck?'

Mandy shook her head. 'No, but they'll put a poster up for us.'

'Let's try Mr Oliver in the butcher's shop,' James suggested.

But they had no luck there either. They asked Ernie Bell who lived in the cottages behind the Fox and Goose but he hadn't seen Charley. Neither had Eileen Davy from the Old School House. Nor grumpy Mr Simmons, clipping the hedge in the churchyard. In fact no one had seen her. By the time they had asked almost everyone they knew, their task seemed hopeless.

'Come on, James,' Mandy said, feeling miserable again. 'Let's get back to Animal Ark and do those posters.'

Back at the cottage, Mandy found some paper

to make the posters. They sat down at the kitchen table.

'If we just do one,' Mandy said, chewing the end of her pen thoughtfully, 'Jean will let us make some photocopies to put up round the village. Any ideas, James?'

'How about this?' James wrote on a piece of scrap paper.

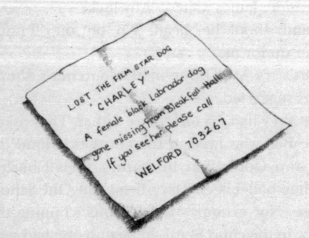

LOST THE FILM STAR DOG
"CHARLEY"
A female black Labrador dog
gone missing from Bleakfell Hall
If you see her please call
WELFORD 703267

'That looks great,' Mandy said delightedly. 'Good old James!'

James went a bit red.

Just then, Mr Hope came into the kitchen. 'What are you up to, you two?' he asked.

'We're making a poster about Charley to put up

round the village,' Mandy explained.

Mr Hope peered over James's shoulder at the poster. 'That's a good idea. Mum told me about Charley – I do hope she turns up.'

'So do we,' they chorused.

'Do you have to do it right now?' Mr Hope asked.

'Well, the sooner the better. Why?' Mandy asked curiously.

'Well, I've got to go up to the animal sanctuary. I thought you might like to come.'

'Mrs Platt's poodle!' Mandy exclaimed. In the worry over Charley she had forgotten all about it.

Adam Hope held up his hand. 'I don't know if they've actually got a poodle, Mandy, but it would be a good chance to ask. Someone's handed in a fox that's been injured; that's why I'm going.'

'Want to come, James?' Mandy said to her friend.

James shook his head. 'I'd like to but I'd better get back. My aunt's coming this afternoon. I could do the poster if you like. Then we could photocopy it when you get back.'

'Oh, James, that would be great.'

James rolled up the paper. 'See you later then,' he said, going out.

'Want to come with us, Jess?' Mandy bent down to stroke Jess, curled up in her basket.

'Leave her,' Mr Hope said. 'She looks tired out.'

Mandy frowned. 'I hope she's OK. She's been looking a bit droopy lately.'

'Hmm.' Mr Hope stroked his beard thoughtfully. 'Remind me, I'll take a look at her when we get back.'

Twenty minutes later Mandy and her father were bumping and rattling their way up the unmade road that led to the animal rescue centre. Mandy stared gloomily out of the window. All she could think of was Charley, running loose somewhere on the moors and dales. In the distance, she could see the far-away lumps of the Pennine Hills. White clouds had built up over their tops like raggy puffs of cotton wool in a clear blue sky.

'What happened to the fox?' Mandy asked, dragging her thoughts away from Charley.

'Caught in one of those wire snares, I'm afraid,' Mr Hope said with a grim look on his face.

Mandy's heart went out to the poor wild creature. 'I hate snares,' she announced angrily. 'They should be banned! I don't know how people can set them.'

They drove through the gate. The big sign said 'Welford Animal Sanctuary' with a picture of a donkey painted in grey.

Betty Hilder, the woman who ran the sanctuary, came out of one of the sheds to greet them. She wore a long floral skirt with a man's tweed jacket over the top and heavy boots. Her face was brown and weathered. A couple of rather skinny cats wound themselves round her legs as she walked.

'Thanks for coming, Adam.' She shook his hand. 'The fox is in the barn. Come and see.'

The injured fox lay in a wire cage in an old stone barn next to a row of kennels. It snarled in fear as they approached.

'I think it's got a broken leg,' Betty said. 'It won't let me near it.'

Mandy bent to look into the cage. She felt angry and upset that the fox had been injured. Why couldn't people just leave wild creatures in peace?

'Here.' As she stood up, Mr Hope handed

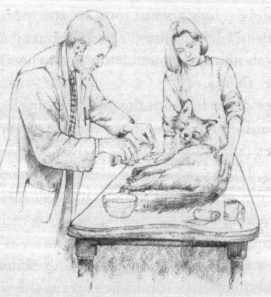

Mandy a strong pair of gloves from his bag. 'Put these on. We'll take a look.'

Mandy held the young fox's head firmly. Its coat was red and glossy with a beautiful white bib. Mr Hope quickly examined its swollen front leg.

'He's been licking it by the looks of it, Dad.' Mandy felt a surge of pity. The fox looked at her with fear in its black eyes.

'Yes. I'm afraid it needs more than just a lick to make it better,' Mr Hope said with a frown on his usually good-humoured face.

'It's OK,' Mandy said gently to the struggling

fox. 'We're not going to hurt you.'

'It's broken all right,' Mr Hope said. 'I'll give him an injection to make him sleep while I strap it up. Could we have a bowl of hot water please, Betty?'

Mandy held on firmly as Mr Hope injected the scared creature with a mild anaesthetic. Gradually, she felt it go limp. Its eyes closed as it fell asleep.

Betty came back with a bowl of steaming water.

'This won't take long.' Mr Hope took a roll of fine white mesh bandage from his bag.

'We soak this in the hot water,' he explained. 'It goes all soft and we wrap it round the broken leg.'

'Then when it dries,' Mandy went on, 'it sets hard, like a plaster.'

'How long will it have to be on there do you think?' Betty asked, after they had finished.

'A few weeks,' Mr Hope said. 'Then he should be as good as new.'

'Thanks, Adam, Mandy.' Betty smiled at them both.

'Keep him warm, plenty to drink.' Mr Hope stroked the glossy red fur while Mandy settled the fox back into its cage.

'How much do I owe you?' Betty asked.

Mr Hope patted Betty's arm. 'Nothing. I had to come up this way anyway.' He winked at Mandy. Her dad never charged the sanctuary. *But don't tell your mum*, the wink seemed to say.

They all went outside.

'Betty,' Mandy said, 'I don't suppose you have a poodle to adopt? Mrs Platt's just had to have hers put to sleep and she can't afford to buy a new one.'

'I'm sorry, we haven't, Mandy. Not at the moment,' Betty said. 'But I'll let you know if we get one.'

'Thanks,' Mandy said. 'Oh, and by the way, if you see a black Labrador, or if anyone brings one in, the film company up at Bleakfell Hall has lost one.'

'Oh, dear,' Betty said. 'Of course. I'll let you know if I hear of anything,' she promised.

Mandy took a last glance back at the rows of kennels as they drove away. She felt sad and angry that there were so many homeless animals in the world.

A couple of miles from the village, the car phone rang.

'Yup,' Mandy heard her dad say. 'Where? I'll tell her. Thanks, Jean.

'Mr Redpath's called Jean to say he's seen a black dog in one of his fields. Apparently it ran off towards the river,' Mr Hope explained.

'Oh, Dad!' Mandy's heart leapt with hope. 'It could be Charley. Did Mr Redpath say if it was wearing a collar?'

'Yes,' Mr Hope glanced at his daughter. 'A red one.'

'Yippee!' Mandy cried, clapping her hands together. 'Oh, Dad, it really could be her.'

Mandy's heart drummed all the way home. Charley was definitely still alive and in the area. It could only be a matter of time before they found her!

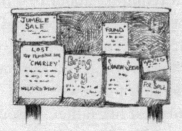

Six

'Can I turn the radio on, Dad?' Mandy asked as they neared the village.

'Yes, of course, Mandy.'

'I phoned Radio Yorkshire. They're going to put out a call for Charley on the afternoon show,' she explained. Mandy switched the radio on just as the show was ending.

'Oh,' Mandy felt disappointed. 'I would have loved to hear what they said.'

The announcer was still talking.

'Shh,' Mr Hope turned up the volume. 'Listen!'

'And just a reminder about that missing dog,' the announcer said. 'Her name's Charley and she's wearing a red collar. If you see her, phone Welford 703627 – there's a very anxious girl waiting desperately for news.'

Mandy looked at her father. 'It sounded great, didn't it?' She felt a surge of hope.

'Yes.' Mr Hope patted Mandy's knee. 'Let's hope it does the trick.'

Back at Animal Ark James was waiting.

'I managed to escape from Mum and my aunt,' he admitted. 'I said this was really urgent.'

'Well, it is.' Mandy told James about Mr Redpath seeing a dog with a red collar.

'It could be Charley!' James said excitedly.

'I know,' Mandy said. 'That's why we've got to get these up quick – so if anyone sees her they'll know who she is.'

James had written the poster in green marker pen with a drawing of a black Labrador on one side.

'Oh, James, it's brilliant! Come on, let's ask Jean if we can use the photocopier.'

They went through into the surgery reception.

Jean Knox was looking through the blue appointment book. She glanced up and smiled as Mandy and James came through.

'Can we use the photocopier please, Jean?' Mandy asked.

Jean took off her glasses. They swung on a silver chain against her hand-knitted pink cardigan. 'What is it, dear?' Jean was a bit fussy about the office machines.

'A poster,' Mandy explained. 'About Charley, the missing film star dog.'

'Yes, help yourselves.'

They went into the back room. The photocopier whirred as Mandy made a dozen copies.

'Where to first?' James asked as they hurried outside.

'I'm going to ask the vicar if we can put one on the parish notice-board,' Mandy said. 'It will be a great place. Everyone who comes to the village has to pass it.'

They made their way across the village green and down the short-cut beside the Fox and Goose. Old Walter Pickard was in the front garden of his little stone cottage, dead-heading his roses. His fat tom-cat was asleep on the front step in a pool of late afternoon sunshine. Walter was an old friend of Grandad's. Both of them had been church bell-ringers for years.

'Now then, you youngsters,' Walter called. 'Where are you off to?'

'Hello, Mr Pickard. We're just going to ask the vicar if he'll put one of these up.' Mandy showed Walter the poster.

'What's that all about then?'

Mandy quickly explained about Charley.

'Is she a star then? I haven't seen her.'

'Well,' Mandy said. 'She's a star to us because she's such a beautiful dog.'

'We thought it would make people take notice,' James added.

'Aye, it will that. Well, good luck, young miss. I'll keep an eye out for her.'

'Thanks, Mr Pickard.'

Outside the church, Mr Hadcroft, Welford's vicar, was just getting off his bicycle.

Mandy and James ran across.

'Well, hello, you two.' The vicar took off his crash-helmet. 'You look in a hurry.'

'Yes, we are a bit.' Mandy had suddenly realised

it was near closing time. In fifteen minutes or so the shops would be shut and the posters would have to wait until tomorrow. Her heart lurched to think Charley had been missing almost a whole day.

'Could you please put this poster up on the board,' Mandy begged. 'We'd be ever so grateful.'

Mr Hadcroft looked at the poster. 'Sure,' he said. He used several rusty drawing pins to pin up the poster. He stood back. 'That looks fine. Hope you have some luck with the dog.'

'Thanks!' Mandy and James chorused. They sprinted across the green to the post office.

Mrs McFarlane was counting the money in the till.

'Here's the poster about Charley,' Mandy said breathlessly.

'Leave it on the counter, dear,' Mrs McFarlane said, putting a pile of ten-pence pieces into a blue bag. 'I'll put it up when I've finished doing the money.'

Mandy and James dashed back to the grocer's, then to the butcher. Soon, every shop in the village had the poster in its window. They even stuck one on the huge oak tree by the village pond.

'Just in time,' James panted as the very last doorbell clanged behind them. 'Now we'll just have to wait to see what happens.'

'I'll phone Bleakfell Hall tonight and tell them what we've done,' said Mandy. 'I've just got time to do my chores before tea.'

At Animal Ark, evening surgery was just beginning. Mandy popped her head round the door.

'We're back,' she said to her mum. Mrs Hope was sitting at the bench counting sterile-packed hypodermic needles. She looked up. 'Where from?'

'We've been putting posters about Charley all round the village.'

'Well done, Mandy.' Mrs Hope replaced the box on the shelf. 'Hope it does the trick.'

As they passed the treatment room Mandy saw Jess up on the table. Mr Hope was just finishing examining her.

'Is she OK, Dad?' Mandy went in to stroke the terrier.

Mr Hope glanced at Mandy's anxious face. 'She's fine, Mandy.' He smiled. 'She's absolutely fine.'

'That's good.' Mandy heaved a sigh of relief. A

missing Labrador and a sick terrier would just be too much to cope with!

Later, after James had gone home for supper, Mandy rang Bleakfell Hall. She was so anxious for news of Charley she had hardly been able to eat a thing.

Luckily, Ben Burton, Mr Curtis's assistant, answered.

'Oh, hello, Mandy. I don't suppose you've heard anything about the dog, have you?'

'No,' Mandy said. 'That's why I'm ringing. I hoped *you* had.'

'No – nothing. And Animal Stars haven't got another black Labrador available. I really don't know what we're going to do!'

Mandy's heart sank. In spite of the posters, the call to the local radio, she had still been holding on to a desperate hope that Charley might find her way back to Bleakfell Hall on her own.

'One of the local farmers saw a black Labrador,' she told Ben. 'I hoped it was Charley but we haven't heard anything since.' She glanced at the clock over the inglenook fireplace. It was eight-thirty, almost twenty-four hours since Charley ran off!

'I know you're upset about her,' Ben was saying, 'but we've got to get on with filming. I don't suppose you know of another dog we could use, Mandy?'

'Well,' Mandy said, an idea occurring to her. 'My friend James has got a black Labrador.'

'Great! Is he obedient?'

'Well . . .' Mandy hesitated. Should she tell a little white lie? James would be so proud if Blackie was in a film. 'Yes, he's not *too* bad.' It wasn't a fib at all, really. Blackie wasn't too bad at doing as he was told. Just not too good, either.

'Could you bring him up? We could give it a try,' Ben said, sounding pleased.

'I should think that'll be OK. I'll ask.'

'Mandy, you're wonderful. Mr Curtis will be so happy.' Ben sounded delighted. 'Can you come tomorrow?'

'I expect so,' Mandy said. 'I'll ring James now if you like. I'm sure my dad will bring us.'

'Fine,' said Ben. 'See you in the morning.'

James was full of excitement when she phoned to tell him what Ben Burton had said.

'I'll get up early and give Blackie a bath,' James said. 'He rolled in some manure this morning so he's not allowed indoors at the moment.'

'Trust him,' Mandy said. She put the phone down with a sigh. It was all very well Blackie being Charley's stand-in. But what they really needed was Charley herself!

Very early next morning James and a super-clean Blackie were on the doorstep.

'Wow! You're early,' Mandy said as she answered James's knock on the door.

'It's not every day Blackie gets his big chance,' James said proudly.

Mr Hope came through from the surgery. 'I'm taking you up to Bleakfell Hall,' he said. 'Mum's busy with surgery this morning. I've just got to load the Land-rover up. We've got to call in at Sunrise Farm on the way – a cow's down with milk-fever.'

When they arrived at Sunrise Farm, Mr Jones, the farmer, came out from the angular grey-stone farmhouse to greet them. He had an empty tobacco-pipe in his mouth. Mandy had never seen him without it. It hissed and bubbled like a kettle as he sucked.

'Make sure Blackie stays in the car,' Mr Hope

warned. 'We don't want the cow getting upset, especially as she has a new calf.'

'Went down early this morning,' Mr Jones explained. *Suck, suck, hiss, bubble.* 'We tried to get her up but it's no good.'

In the barn, a cream and brown Jersey cow was lying in the straw. Her legs were folded up underneath her stomach. They had propped her up with a couple of straw bales to stop her rolling over. By her side stood a soft-eyed calf barely more than a few hours old. It mooed softly and wobbled away on unsteady legs. There was a sweet smell of fresh milk and hay.

Mr Hope knelt down beside the mother cow. He ran his hands over her flanks.

'OK, old girl,' he said. 'We'll soon have you on your feet.'

Mandy knew what was needed. 'Shall I get the bottle of calcium from your bag, Dad?'

'Yes, please, Mandy. And a needle and a tube.'

'Milk-fever's caused by a sudden loss of calcium,' Mr Hope explained to a wide-eyed James. 'It happens soon after a new calf is born. I'll inject some calcium into the cow and she'll soon be as good as new.'

Mr Hope took the needle from Mandy and attached it to a long, thin rubber tube. Then he fixed the other end to a bottle. He quickly stuck the needle into one of the cow's veins.

'Hold it up please, Mandy.'

As the calcium flowed into the cow's blood, she began to stir. After a while Mr Hope pulled out the needle. He wiped his hands on his overalls.

'OK, stand back, she's going to get up.'

Mandy held her breath. The cow struggled to her feet. Mandy's heart pounded. Would the cow fall again? She had helped her father do this many times and knew it was always an anxious moment.

The mother cow was swaying about in the sun-yellow straw like a great ship on the sea. Then she seemed to get her balance. She moved forward as her calf came trotting. She mooed softly. A new sucking noise came as the calf greedily drank its mother's milk.

Mandy breathed a sigh of relief. It was times like this, knowing she could really help to save an animal's life, that made her more keen than ever to be a vet herself.

'Thanks, Adam.' Mr Jones looked relieved.

Suck, suck, bubble, bubble went his empty pipe. 'I can't afford to lose such a good milker. Well done, Mandy. I can see you're going to make a great vet yourself one day.' *Bubble . . . bubble . . .*

Mandy blushed with pride.

'We're on our way to Bleakfell Hall,' Mandy heard her father say.

'Any sign of their missing dog? I heard about it when I went into the post office yesterday,' Mr Jones said.

'Not yet. We're keeping our fingers crossed. In the meantime James's dog is going to act as a stand-in.'

The farmer grinned then sucked even harder on his empty pipe. 'Good luck!'

But things didn't quite go as Mandy expected.

As they drew up outside Bleakfell Hall, the front door suddenly flew open. Out surged a stream of people led by a woman in a white silk frock.

'That's Antonia Kent,' Mandy whispered to her father. 'What's happened now?'

Antonia Kent strode towards them in a swathe of silk. After her ran Hammond Curtis, clipboard held aloft. Today, a red bandana replaced his

usual baseball cap. After *him* ran Ben Burton, holding out what looked like a mug of tea. Next came one of the production assistants. Then Mandy gasped with surprise as a man in an old-fashioned frock coat and top hat came running out. His white shirt was covered in blood. Sticking out from his chest was a ruby handled dagger although he was striding along like a healthy athlete.

Last but not least, there was a flurry of red and green. Mr Baggins the parrot!

'Mr Baggins.' Mandy climbed hastily from the Land-rover. She ran towards the parrot. 'Mr Baggins!'

With a screech the bright bird flew over Antonia's head. She crouched down on the driveway, hands waving like a windmill.

'Beastly thing! Take it away, someone!'

'*Good morning!*' Mr Baggins screeched. '*Where's Charley?*' With that he promptly landed on Mandy's head.

'There you are,' Miss Kent said dramatically. Her nose was up in the air, her wig falling over one eye. 'If this girl's so good with animals, *she* can star in this dreadful film. I'm leaving!'

Seven

'What on earth's going on?' Mr Hope's mouth fell open when he saw the procession of people pour out of Bleakfell Hall.

'Come down, Mr Baggins,' Mandy commanded. The naughty parrot stepped on to her fingers. Then he hopped off on to her shoulder.

'*Where's the cup tea. I wanna be a yeah, yeah,*' Mr Baggins murmured in her ear.

The director, Hammond Curtis, was trying to soothe Antonia Kent with a mug of tea. They were sitting on the stone steps, talking earnestly.

'I'm sure the parrot will behave itself now Mandy's here,' Mr Curtis was saying. Mandy saw him wink at her over the actress's shoulder.

'He tried to peck my beauty spot.' Antonia sniffed, wiping her eyes.

'He thought it was a sunflower seed – now please calm down, Antonia.' Mr Curtis patted Antonia Kent's shaking shoulder.

Mandy tried not to laugh out loud. 'We've brought Blackie,' she managed to splutter.

Mr Hope had gone round to the stables to look at one of the horses that had gone lame. Blackie was sitting, good as gold, at James's feet.

Suddenly Mr Curtis stood up. He clapped his hands. 'OK, everyone, back inside. I've managed to persuade Miss Kent to carry on and Charley's understudy has arrived by the look of it. Let's get on with the job, shall we?'

They all filed back indoors. Mr Curtis waited for Mandy and James.

'This is Blackie, is it?' He gave the dog a pat. 'Thanks for bringing him, young man.'

'That's OK,' James mumbled shyly.

'I hope he's going to be obedient.'

'Oh, no – yes, I mean.' James went red.

'I expect he will,' Mandy said hastily. 'For the first time ever,' she whispered under her breath.

'I've been training him,' James said, looking up at Mr Curtis.

'Good man.' Mr Curtis slapped James on the shoulder.

Suddenly, with a squawk Mr Baggins took off. Up into the chandelier. A screech filled the air.

Mandy heard a groan from the crew.

'OK, OK,' Mr Curtis shouted. 'Leave him there for the time being.'

Someone stepped forward with a black and white clapperboard.

'Take your places!' Mr Curtis ordered.

The man with the dagger in his chest lay backwards on the hall table. Someone ran over with a bottle. He splashed gooey red liquid on the floor.

'Not too much,' Mr Curtis called. 'It's not a horror film.'

He beckoned to James. 'Can you get your dog to lie by the fireplace, young man?'

'I'll try,' James said.

Mandy held her breath. She suddenly

remembered all the trouble Blackie had caused at this year's Welford Show, snatching Mrs Ponsonby's hat and running riot in the show ring. 'Oh, Blackie,' she whispered. 'Please be good!'

James led Blackie towards the big stone fireplace. He unclipped his lead. 'Stay!' he commanded. James fished about in the pocket of his track suit trousers. He held up a biscuit. 'Stay!' he commanded again.

Blackie lay down, head on paws. His eyes roamed the room. Mandy's heart was in her mouth.

Blackie stared up at Mr Baggins. Mr Baggins

stared down at Blackie. James backed away from the dog, hand raised. Blackie lay still. *It's going to be all right*, Mandy thought. *It's really going to be all right!*

Ben took Mandy aside. 'This is the scene just after the murder,' he whispered. 'Blackie . . . er, Black Rose and Mr Baggins are the only witnesses.'

'Oh,' Mandy whispered. Miss Kent looked angry enough to stab someone for real.

'Then she removes the dagger and hides it in the cupboard. But Black Rose sniffs it out.'

'Oh, dear!' Mandy's eyes were wide. 'I'm not sure . . .'

'What?' Ben asked.

'Nothing,' Mandy said. She thought perhaps it was the wrong time to tell Ben that the only thing Blackie was good at sniffing out was his dinner!

'We got to this bit before you arrived,' Ben went on. 'But Mr Baggins took a sudden fancy to that beauty spot on Antonia Kent's cheek.'

Mandy giggled. She wouldn't have missed this for anything!

'Silence!' Mr Curtis yelled.

Antonia Kent took her position by the corpse. The clapperboard clapped.

They were ready.

Antonia Kent pretended to look round warily. Then, still glancing over her shoulder, she began to remove the dagger from the man's chest.

A sudden commotion from the first floor landing made her freeze in her tracks. The three cats came hurtling down the staircase. In front, a little grey mouse fled in terror. They sped across the hall and through the door.

Mr Baggins squawked in alarm. '*She loves tea!*' he screeched. '*Where's Charley?*'

Antonia Kent screamed. 'A mouse . . . a mouse!' Up went her long skirts. She jumped on to the table in one great leap.

It was all too much for Blackie. First the parrot; then the cats; now a screaming, jumping woman. He barked, leapt to his feet, hared after the cats. His claws scratched the wooden floor as he slipped and scrambled his way to the kitchen.

'Cut!' Mr Curtis yelled.

Mandy snorted with laughter. Mr Curtis put his head into his hands. The man with the dagger in his chest stood up and lit a cigarette. In one corner, a young woman dressed as a Victorian parlour-maid took a can of Coke from behind a potted plant and raised it to her lips.

Mandy wiped her eyes. James disappeared towards the kitchen after Blackie. Ben Burton was doubled up, laughing his head off. Antonia Kent swept up the stairs in a flurry of long skirts and hurt pride. The scene was ruined.

Mandy ran after James.

In the kitchen, George Sims had hold of Blackie's collar. The Labrador was sitting at his feet, looking sorry for himself. James was telling him off.

'Blackie!' He shook his finger at the dog. Mr Sims let go of his collar and Blackie lay down beside him.

George Sims scratched his head. 'I thought it was Charley coming through that door,' he said.

'I'm afraid not.' Mandy gave Blackie a hug. He might not be a good actor, but he was a great one for cheering people up. She looked up at Mr Sims. 'No sign of Charley, then?'

Mr Sims shook his head. 'If she don't turn up soon. I'm likely to lose my job,' he said, looking sorry for himself.

'We put a call out on the local radio,' Mandy said. 'And put posters up in the village.'

'Well, thanks for your help,' Mr Sims said gruffly. 'I know I was daft to let her out. I'm just not used to animals.'

'When are they sending your replacement?' Mandy began to feel sorry for George Sims. He really wasn't so bad. And she could see by the look on his face that he would never have frightened Charley on purpose.

Mr Sims shrugged. 'Tomorrow, I hope. There's something wrong with one of the horses now. I thought parrots were enough trouble.' He shook his head. 'I just can't cope with it. If I didn't have a wife and four kids, I'd quit the job.'

Mandy suddenly had an idea. 'Mr Sims,' she said. 'If you like, James and I will help out with the animals. Just until the new person comes that is.'

George Sims seemed to cheer up a bit. A grin spread across his face. 'Now, that's not a bad idea. Them horses need mucking out but—' His face fell. '—I couldn't pay you anything.'

Mandy waved her hand. 'No, we wouldn't want paying, would we, James?'

'Er . . . no,' James said, although Mandy didn't think he looked very certain.

George Sims beamed. 'All right, you're on.' He looked over his shoulder. 'I expect I could run to getting you a few ice creams.'

Mandy grinned. 'Thanks, Mr Sims.'

Just then, Hammond Curtis came into the kitchen. Mr Baggins sat on his shoulder. Mandy only just managed to suppress a giggle. Mr Curtis only needed a wooden leg and an eye patch and he'd look like Long John Silver!

'I think everyone's calmed down now,' he said. 'Thanks for bringing your dog, James. I'm sorry, I don't think he'll be suitable after all.'

James's face fell. 'I am *trying* to train him, honestly.'

Mandy felt sorry for James – and for Blackie. He'd lost his big chance to be a star.

'Of course, what we really need,' Mr Curtis said, glaring at George Sims, 'is Charley! If she's not found, I don't know *what* we're going to do!'

Mr Sims hung his head.

Mr Curtis put Mr Baggins back on his perch. 'You'd better round up the cats, George. Goodness knows where they've all got to.'

'And we'll go and find my dad, and ask him if we can stay and help with the animals,' Mandy said.

Mr Hope was just washing his hands under the yard tap.

'Dad,' Mandy said excitedly. 'We're going to stay and help George. Is that OK?'

'Yes, of course it is. I'll pick you up later if you like. How did Blackie's debut go?'

James blushed. 'He failed his audition.'

'Oh, dear.' Mr Hope's eyes twinkled. 'I must say I'm not surprised. That dog's too intelligent to let anyone boss him around.'

James brightened. 'That's right,' he said proudly. 'Thank you, Mr Hope.'

A couple of hours later everything was spick and span. Mandy and James had mucked out and put clean bedding in the stables. They had fed the horses, and the cats, which they'd found in the cellar standing guard over a mouse-hole in the skirting-board. James had swept the yard while Mandy sat by the fire in the kitchen grooming the cats. She giggled, thinking about Blackie and Mr Baggins and poor Antonia Kent. How could anyone be scared of a tiny little mouse?

When Mr Hope arrived to collect them, Mandy and James were eating ice creams in the kitchen. Mr Baggins was asleep, his head tucked under his wing.

'Don't know what I'd have done without them.' George Sims said as Mr Hope came through the door. 'They can work for Animal Stars any time!'

'Can we come back tomorrow, Dad?' Mandy asked.

'Yes, fine. I've got to go to Walton Market in the afternoon. I'll drop you off on the way,' Mr Hope said.

'Thanks, Dad.' Mandy's eyes shone. 'You're the best.'

'*Where's the tea?*' Mr Baggins mumbled sleepily.

Mr Hope dropped James and Blackie off at their gate on the way back to Animal Ark.

'See you tomorrow, James,' Mandy called, waving goodbye.

When they arrived home, Mr Hope went off to make out his report. Mandy greeted Jess in the kitchen. The terrier was in her basket. She looked up and wagged her tail as Mandy came in but didn't climb out. Mandy frowned. Jess really was out of sorts lately. She hoped her dad had been right when he said she was OK.

'A long walk might be what you need, Jess,' Mandy said, stroking her wiry coat. 'You're not getting enough exercise, that's the trouble. I'll take you in the morning if you're good.'

She gave the dog a hug then went through into the surgery. Simon was sterilising the surgical instruments.

'Oh, Mandy,' he said as she came in. 'There was a telephone call for you.'

'Who from?' Mandy asked curiously.

'I don't know – ask Jean.' Simon opened the steriliser to a cloud of steam.

Mandy went through to reception. Jean was sitting at her typewriter, a frown on her face. She was trying to work out Mr Hope's spidery handwriting on a sheet of paper beside her machine.

'Jean, Simon says there was a call for me,' Mandy said eagerly.

'Oh, yes.' Jean flicked through her shorthand pad. '. . . Here it is. Betty from the animal sanctuary. She asked you to call her.'

Mandy's heart leapt. It might be news about Charley!

'Use my phone if you like,' Jean went on. 'The sanctuary's number is on the notice-board above your head.'

Mandy was so excited she could hardly dial the number.

'Animal sanctuary, Betty speaking.'

'Betty,' Mandy said breathlessly. 'There's a message for me to ring you.'

Betty recognised her voice. 'Hi, Mandy,' she said cheerfully. 'I thought you'd like to know the RSPCA have brought in a stray poodle. She might do for your friend, Mrs Platt.'

'That's great, Betty,' Mandy said, brushing aside her disappointment at there being no news of Charley. 'Could we come up and see her?'

'Yes, sure,' Betty replied. 'Whenever you like.'

'I'll ask if Mum or Dad can bring me. We'll come as soon as we can.'

'OK, Mandy. I'll be here,' said Betty.

Mandy put the phone down. She looked at her watch. If her mum wasn't busy she just might take her up to the sanctuary before surgery.

Mandy hurried through into the kitchen. Mrs Hope was folding her white vet's coat.

'Mum!' Mandy burst out. 'Is there time for us

to go up to the animal sanctuary before surgery?'

Mrs Hope glanced up at the clock. 'Yes, I should think so. Why?'

'Betty's just phoned. She's got a poodle for Mrs Platt. Can we go and see her?'

Mrs Hope put her vet's coat on the shelf. 'That's great news. I'll just get my keys.'

She came back a minute later. 'Come on then, sweetheart. Let's go and take a look at this poodle.'

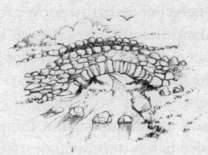

Eight

Mandy fidgeted all the way to the animal sanctuary. Her eyes darted from side to side, as they drove along, still looking for signs of Charley. To find Charley and a poodle for Mrs Platt all in one day would be like a dream come true.

At the animal sanctuary, Betty ushered them into the house. The poodle, thin and weak, lay in a basket in front of Betty's fire.

'Oh . . .' Mandy knelt down beside the basket. She gently touched the poodle's matted grey coat.

Her heart turned over with pity.

'She had been left tied to a tree over at Monkton Spinney,' Mandy heard Betty saying to Mrs Hope. 'Luckily someone spotted her and took her to the RSPCA. She probably wouldn't have survived another night.'

'How could anyone do such a thing!' Mandy said, her voice barely a whisper.

She heard her mother sigh. 'Don't ask me, Mandy. I don't know either.'

Mandy looked up at Betty and her mother. They were standing watching her stroke the poodle. Mrs Hope's face was full of sadness.

'Do you think she'll be OK, Mum?' Mandy asked anxiously. She had seen abandoned animals before but never one who looked quite so thin and ill.

Her mother crouched down beside her. She quickly ran her hands over the little dog then looked into her eyes and ears.

'It's hard to say,' said Mrs Hope. 'She's suffering from exposure.' She lifted the dog's muzzle to look at her teeth. 'A few good meals and a day or so in the warm and we'll take another look at her, OK?'

'Oh, *thanks*, Mum.' Mandy gave her mother a hug. 'She's got to be OK, she's just got to be!'

Mandy stroked the poodle gently. It raised its head weakly and licked her hand.

'There you are!' Mandy stood up. 'I know she's a little fighter!'

'She's had some warm milk and cereal,' said Betty. 'And what she really needs too is lots of love.'

'Mrs Platt will give her that, won't she, Mum?' Mandy said, trying to imagine Mrs Platt's delighted face when they turned up with a new dog for her.

'She certainly will,' Mrs Hope said. 'But, Mandy, I think we'd better make sure the dog is going to get really well before we tell Mrs Platt.'

'Whatever you say, Mum. I'll come up and see her again. I'll bring my pocket money next time. It will help pay for her food.'

'That is kind, Mandy,' Betty gave her a hug.

They left the poodle lying in her warm basket and went outside.

'I'm sorry, Mandy,' Mrs Hope said. 'We must get back. It's time for surgery.'

They waved goodbye to Betty and set off towards

Welford. Along the lane, Mrs Hope slowed down while two girl riders trotted past.

'Hello, Mrs Hope,' one of the girls called. It was Susan Collins, a new girl in the area. She had had a difficult time settling in at first, but she now looked completely at home.

Mrs Hope wound down her window. 'Hello, Susan. How's Prince these days?'

'Fine thank you,' Susan replied.

Mandy waved as the girls trotted smartly on.

For the rest of the journey home, Mandy was very thoughtful.

'You're quiet, Mandy,' Mrs Hope remarked.

'I was just thinking about Charley and that little poodle,' she said gloomily. 'Sometimes I think I'll never make a good vet – I get too upset.'

Mrs Hope patted her daughter's knee. 'Yes, you will, Mandy. I know you will. You'd make a very *bad* vet if you didn't care about your patients.'

Mandy sniffed, feeling a bit better. 'Yes, I suppose you're right.' She thought for a minute. She smiled at her mother. Mum always had the knack of saying the right thing. 'You know, Mum,' Mandy said, 'I think I'll call the poodle Antonia.'

Mrs Hope smiled. 'That's a very grand name. Why Antonia?'

'After that actress at Bleakfell Hall. She reminds me of a poodle with her hair tied up on the top of her head like that.'

'That's a bit cheeky, Mandy,' Mrs Hope said.

'No it's not,' Mandy replied indignantly. 'Poodles are beautiful. I think it's a compliment!'

The following morning, Mandy was putting out food for her rabbits when James arrived with Blackie. They were off on that walk Mandy had promised Jess.

The terrier barked with joy at seeing Blackie. The two dogs greeted each other with sniffs and wagging tails then ran off, chasing madly round and round the lawn.

'Mind the plants!' Mandy called. 'Control your dog, James!' she said with a grin.

'Some hope,' James muttered. He whistled to Blackie but the Labrador ignored him as usual.

'Where shall we go for our walk?' Mandy asked.

James shrugged. 'Up to you.'

They went into the kitchen to fetch Jess's lead. Mr Hope was reading his veterinary magazine at the table.

'Where are you two off to?' he asked as they came through the door.

'We're taking Jess on a long walk to try to get rid of that fat tummy.' Mandy bent to hug the Jack Russell.

Mr Hope shut his magazine and rose from the table. 'Well, I must go. I've got several calls to make. Mind how you go, you two. Take good care of Jess.'

Mandy frowned as her father went out. That was a funny thing to say. He *knew* she always took great care of the little Jack Russell. Mandy shrugged. Oh, well, her dad did say funny things sometimes. She took Jess's lead from its hook.

'Come on, you two.' Blackie and Jess were wagging their tails at each other and panting after their race round the garden. 'Let's go.'

They walked along the lane to the post office.

'I'm just going to get some penny chews.' James produced a ten-pence piece from his pocket.

They tied the dogs up outside.

'Hello, you two,' Mr McFarlane said from behind the counter. 'Any news of that dog from Bleakfell Hall yet, Mandy?'

Mandy shook her head sadly. 'Not yet, but we're keeping our fingers crossed.'

Outside, James gave Mandy five penny chews and they set off across the village green. Jess and Blackie strained at their leads.

'Let's go past the War Memorial,' Mandy said, pulling Jess back. 'Down by the pub and along the river. We can let them off along there.'

'Great,' James said.

They stopped briefly on the bridge to throw sticks into the river, then they climbed over the stile and wandered down to the river's edge. Mandy loved the sound of the water as it sang and bubbled over the stones. The level was high, swollen from last week's rain. Mandy unclipped Jess's lead.

'Off you go – and stay where we can see you!' she said sternly.

Jess bounded off, Blackie at her heels. They sniffed along the bank, darting to and fro as they caught the scent of a rabbit.

Suddenly, Mandy saw Jess scramble down to the river's edge. Blackie followed, his tail waving like a flag.

Then, all at once, Mandy saw Jess stand stock-still. Her head was cocked to one side.

'What's Jess heard?' James asked.

Mandy frowned. 'I don't know. Let's go and see.'

They scrambled down the bank. Mandy saw the alert little terrier standing like a statue at the water's edge.

Suddenly, Jess shot forward like a rocket.

'Hey!' Mandy yelled. She felt frightened that Jess might run off, and one missing dog was quite enough! 'Jess! Jess!' she shouted. 'Come back!'

But the terrier ignored her. She splashed across the stepping-stones and scrambled madly up the high bank on the other side of the river.

'Come on, James,' Mandy said urgently. 'We'd better go after her.'

James whistled to Blackie. The Labrador bounded towards him. For once it seemed Blackie was going to be obedient. Then he saw Jess's white tail disappearing over the top of the bank.

He gave a couple of loud barks and set off after her.

'Blackie!' James cried. He turned, but Mandy was already clambering down the bank, across the stepping-stones and up the hill on the other side.

'Wait for me!' he called, running after her.

'Come on,' she called. Her heart was pounding as she ran. 'Jess! Jess!'

By now both dogs had disappeared. Gone!

Through the spinney there was no sign of either of them. A rock-strewn hill lay ahead.

Side by side, Mandy and James scrambled up the hill after the dogs. At the top, they stood on a huge outcrop of rock. Below, the houses in the village looked small, like a doll's town.

Mandy listened. All she could hear was the faraway sound of a train. Surely Jess wouldn't be chasing that? She whirled round, looking in all directions. There was no sign of either dog. Where on earth had they gone?

Then, from behind a distant boulder, Mandy suddenly heard Jess's short, sharp bark.

She jumped down. 'Come on, James, this way!'

They ran towards the sound of Jess's frantic

barks. They dashed across the turf, scrambling over rocks.

'They're over there.' James pointed. 'Look – Blackie's tail is sticking out from behind that rock!'

'Oh, thank goodness.' Mandy heaved a sigh of relief. Now they could hear Jess and see Blackie's waving tail, she was beginning to feel a bit angry with the naughty dogs. Jess would get a good telling-off when they finally caught up with her.

Behind the rock, Jess still barked. A high, excited kind of bark that Mandy had never heard before.

They ran round the other side, then stopped dead in their tracks.

'Oh!' Mandy stood, hand over her mouth in disbelief.

For there, lying on her side beside a big grey boulder, was Charley! Her hind leg was caught in a snare.

Mandy's heart missed a beat. She could hardly believe what she was seeing.

Charley's sad eyes looked up at her as if to say 'Am I glad to see you!'

Mandy fell to her knees. Her throat felt choked

with joy and relief. 'Charley . . . Charley . . .' She blinked back tears.

The dog's back leg was bleeding where the tight wire held it fast. Mandy touched her gently. Charley wagged her tail and licked Mandy's hand. She tried to get up but fell back as the sharp wire dug deeper into her leg. Mandy gasped as she saw the blood ooze.

'Oh, poor Charley!' She looked up at James, her heart filled with anger and pity.

'What are we going to do?' James gulped, kneeling quickly beside Mandy. Jess and Blackie were lying down, panting from their run.

Mandy wrenched off her jacket and lay it over the dog to keep her warm.

Mandy knew they had to get help. They would never manage to carry Charley back themselves. 'I'm going to find Mum or Dad,' she said quickly, her heart thumping in her chest. 'Stay with her, James. Keep Jess and Blackie with you.' She thrust the dog leads at him.

Mandy sped away. The wind blew back her short hair. She flew down the hill as fast as her legs would carry her. She splashed over the stepping-stones, heedless of wet feet and the chilly wind blowing through her sweatshirt. Mandy's breath came out in gasps. Past the village hall, the shops . . . the sleepy morning high street. Her heart seemed to be drumming, *hurry . . . hurry.*

She reached Animal Ark, thrust open the gate and dashed down the front path. She burst into the reception area. The door hit the wall with a clang.

'Where's Dad . . . Mum . . . Simon . . . anyone?' she panted to a startled Jean Knox.

Jean dropped her spectacles in surprise. 'Mandy, what on earth's happened? You look—'

'Please . . . where's . . .' She was completely out of breath.

'Your dad's just got back. He's in his surgery, but—'

Mandy didn't wait to hear any more. She rushed through to the back room.

Mr Hope was filling his bag with veterinary supplies.

'Dad! Dad! You've got to come. Quick!' Mandy gasped. 'We've found Charley!'

Mr Hope's eyes widened in surprise. 'Charley? Where is she?' As he was speaking, he closed his bag quickly and grabbed his car keys from the shelf.

Mandy tugged his arm. 'Quickly . . . oh, please. She's up on the hill. I'll show you as we go.'

They both ran through reception and out of the front door.

'If there's any calls I'll be back soon,' Mr Hope shouted to Jean Knox as they raced down the path.

They both leapt into the Land-rover.

'We went over the stile by the stone bridge,' Mandy explained. 'Jess ran off – she must have heard Charley whining.' Mandy felt so upset she began to sob. 'Oh, Dad, her leg's caught in a snare – it's horrible. Poor Charley.'

Mr Hope was bent over the wheel. The Land-rover roared up the high street and out towards the bridge. Mandy twisted her hands together anxiously. 'Dad, hurry . . . please hurry!'

Nine

Mr Hope screeched to a halt on the bridge. They both leapt out, clambered quickly over the stile and ran along the riverbank.

'This way,' Mandy panted as she plunged down the bank and splashed across the stepping-stones. She began the steep climb up the other side.

'Hang on!' her father called. Mandy was way ahead.

Mandy stopped and turned impatiently. 'Come *on*, Dad, for goodness' sake!' She held out her hand. Her father took it and together they ran through the spinney, out the other side and on up the steep bank towards the place where Charley lay injured.

'How much farther?' Mr Hope panted.

'Just there!' Mandy pointed to the pile of boulders past the steep outcrop of rock. 'Charley's over there!'

At the sound of her voice, Jess and Blackie came bounding up. Jess barked madly, jumping up at Mandy as she ran.

Mandy and Mr Hope arrived at last, breathless and flushed with running all the way from the road.

James leapt to his feet, looking mighty relieved. 'I thought you were never coming!'

'We've been as quick as we could,' Mandy panted.

Mr Hope knelt beside the injured Labrador. Charley wagged her tail feebly and whined. Mandy knelt beside them, clasping her hands together anxiously.

'Now then, old girl,' Mr Hope said gently. 'Let's have a look at you.' He eyed the snare with disgust. 'Who on earth . . . ?'

James shrugged. 'Don't ask me,' he said. 'Some idiot, I expect.'

Mr Hope took pliers from his bag. A couple of quick snips . . . the wire was gone.

'She's been trying to bite it off,' Mr Hope said almost to himself as he examined the wound.

'How long do you think she's been here, Dad?' Mandy felt better now her father was here. If anyone could make Charley OK, he could.

Mr Hope shook his head. 'Not that long – thank goodness. She's a bit thin. Been out on the moors, I should think. It's my guess she was heading back to the village. If she'd been here all the time I'm afraid she'd be dead by now.'

He quickly covered the wound with a rough bandage. 'That'll keep it clean while we carry her back to the car,' he said. 'I'll dress it properly when we get her to the Ark.'

Mr Hope fastened his bag and handed it to Mandy. 'Here, you carry this. He put his arms under the injured dog and lifted her up. She lay quietly in his arms. Her head lolled to one side. Big brown eyes looked at Mandy. Her tail wagged feebly. 'You lead, James,' said Mr Hope.

They set off down the hill in single file. James in front, Mandy behind, her heart pounding anxiously.

A couple of times, Mr Hope slipped on the damp turf. Mandy gasped and dashed forward to steady him, afraid he would stumble and fall with Charley in his arms. After that, she stuck beside her father like glue, guiding him over the uneven ground.

In front, Blackie and Jess trotted beside James as good as gold. Mandy was sure that somehow they realised the seriousness of the situation.

Crossing the river was worse. The stones were slippery at the best of times without having to carry a heavy dog in your arms. Mr Hope couldn't see where he was treading and Mandy had to hold his arm to guide him across. He walked forward hesitantly, putting one foot in front of the other slowly to feel for the stepping-stones. Once, he slipped, his foot going with a splash into the rushing water. Mandy gasped, her heart in her mouth.

Mandy heard her father mutter something under his breath as he fought to regain his balance. Steady at last, he stumbled on across. Mandy was never so glad to feel her feet on dry ground once more.

They scrambled up the bank and walked quickly along to the stile. Mandy helped her father over.

At last they reached the Land-rover. Mandy opened the tail-gate and Mr Hope placed Charley gently inside.

Mandy climbed in with her. 'I'll stay in the back,' she said. Now that Charley had been found, Mandy didn't want to leave her side for a minute.

James and the other two dogs clambered into the front of the vehicle. Mr Hope drove slowly and carefully home.

'I'll phone Bleakfell Hall when we get back, if you like,' James offered. 'Tell them we've found her.'

'Thanks, James,' Mandy said gratefully. 'They'll be so pleased.' She held Charley's head in her lap. The dog looked up at her then licked her hand.

When they arrived at Animal Ark, Mr Hope took Charley directly into the surgery. Mandy held her head while her father bathed and dressed Charley's wounded leg and gave her an injection of antibiotics.

'Will she be all right, Dad?' Mandy asked anxiously.

'She'll be fine. The wound's not very deep, thank goodness.'

James went off to phone the Hall with the good news. 'Ben's pleased as anything,' he said, coming back into the surgery. 'He's going to tell the others.'

Mr Hope carried Charley into the kitchen. He put her down on the floor. Jess came over to lick the Labrador's face. Charley hobbled towards the fire and into Jess's basket

'Oh!' Mandy laughed. 'Sorry, Jess . . . it looks as if you've lost your bed.'

But Jess wouldn't have it. She climbed in and curled up beside Charley.

'Make her a bowl of warm milk and biscuits,' Mr Hope suggested. 'She can have some meat later on.'

Mandy warmed a saucepan of milk on the stove and poured it over a bowl of dog meal. She took it across to Charley. The Labrador lapped it up hungrily, licking the bowl clean in just a few seconds.

'That's better,' Mandy said, stroking Charley's head. 'Now try to get some rest. Come on,' she said to James. 'Let's leave them both to have a good sleep. They deserve it.'

Later that afternoon, after James had gone home, Charley had visitors. Mandy went to answer the knock at the door. Hammond Curtis stood there with Ben Burton and Antonia Kent. Behind them stood George Sims.

Mandy invited them through into the kitchen. George Sims crouched down beside the dog basket. Mandy was pleased when Charley wagged her tail at him. He patted her head awkwardly.

'I should tell you off,' he said gruffly. 'But I suppose it was my fault you ran away.' Charley sniffed the sleeve of his jacket. He patted her head again then stood up. 'Thanks, young lady,' he said. 'I'm very grateful.'

Mandy blushed. 'It's all right, Mr Sims,' she said. 'Jess did it, really.' Mr Sims patted Jess's head.

'The new trainer's arriving later today,' Ben

said. 'George is going to pick her up at the station before he leaves.'

Mr Hope came in from the garden. He shook hands with Mr Curtis and Ben. Antonia Kent offered her cheek to him for a kiss. Mandy almost giggled as her dad looked a bit flustered.

'How long will it be before Charley can work again?' Mr Curtis asked.

'Next week, I should think,' Mr Hope replied. 'She'll limp for a while, but not badly.'

'Can we leave her here for you to look after, Mandy?' Mr Curtis asked. 'The new trainer's coming today but I'd be happier if Charley stayed with you.' He winked at Mandy.

'Well . . .' Mr Hope's eyes twinkled as he looked at his daughter. 'I suppose it will be all right.'

Everyone laughed as Mandy threw her arms round her father's neck. Her heart brimmed with joy as she kissed him soundly on the cheek. She felt honoured to be trusted with a film star dog!

'We'll get on with the scenes she doesn't appear in,' Mr Curtis said, looking relieved. 'But as soon as she's better, it's back to work.'

Antonia Kent opened her handbag. She took out a black and white photograph of herself dressed in the white silk frock she wore in the murder mystery. She took a pen and quickly signed it.

'Here you are, darling.' She thrust the picture in front of Mandy. 'Have this for your dressing-table.'

'Oh!' Mandy said. 'It's great. Thank you, Miss Kent. My friends at school will be really envious.'

Mr Curtis clapped his hands. 'OK, everyone. Back to work.'

'Slave driver,' Antonia Kent said, giving Mandy a wink behind Mr Curtis's back.

Charley and Jess barked goodbye.

A little over a week later, Charley was ready to go back to work.

That afternoon, Mandy rushed out of school as fast as she could. She was in a terrible hurry. There were chores to do, English homework – and maths – and she had to make Charley look beautiful for her return to Bleakfell Hall.

'Hey, what's the rush?' James called as Mandy jumped on her bike and pedalled furiously away from the school gates.

'It's Charley's last day at Animal Ark,' Mandy called over her shoulder. Her schoolbag bumped on her back. 'I've got to get her ready. We're taking her back this evening.'

'Well, you could at least wait for me!' James yelled as Mandy got further and further away.

Mandy waited for him to catch up.

'She looks great,' Mandy said. 'Her leg's healed up beautifully.' She suddenly felt sad. 'Jess is going to miss her like anything.'

'She'll be going back home in a few weeks too,' James reminded her.

'I know,' Mandy said sadly. Animal Ark would seem really empty without Jess and Charley.

They pedalled the two miles to Welford in no time at all. James stopped by Mandy's gate.

'Good luck for tonight,' he said.

Mandy smiled. 'Thanks. I'll feel really upset taking her back,' she confessed.

'You can always borrow Blackie,' James said generously.

Mandy managed a cheerful smile. She squared her shoulders. It was no good moping around. There'd be lots of other animals who needed her help. 'Thanks, James,' she said warmly.

'See you tomorrow!' James waved and pedalled off down the lane.

Mandy left her bike by the shed and went into the kitchen. Charley got up from her place by the fire and came to greet her. Mandy threw her bag down and gave the dog a hug. She looked into the deep brown eyes.

'You look great, Charley. But it's back to work for you, I'm afraid.'

Charley barked.

Mandy looked round. 'Where's Jess?' Suddenly, she heard a strange noise from the broom cupboard. A kind of snuffling, then a tearing noise. Something fell with a clatter and all at once Jess appeared with a yellow duster in her mouth. She let it drop to the floor, put her front paw on it then started trying to tear it up.

Mandy burst out laughing. 'Oh, Jess, you are funny.' She picked Jess up and prised the duster away from her. She hugged her close. 'You're a real monkey.' Mandy suddenly noticed just how tubby the terrier was. She had been so busy looking after Charley during the week that she really hadn't paid much attention to Jess.

Mandy put Jess on the table and felt her tummy.

Underneath she was a bit swollen. Mandy frowned. She knew it was silly but it really looked as if Jess . . .

Just then Mrs Hope came into the kitchen.

'Mandy,' she said with a smile on her face. 'Betty's outside in the car. She's got a surprise for you.'

Mandy's heart leapt. A surprise . . . That could only mean one thing: the poodle. She quickly put Jess down on the floor and ran outside.

Betty stood beside her old station wagon. And beside Betty, on a brand new blue lead with a blue leather collar, stood Antonia, the poodle. She wagged her tail when she saw Mandy run out. Mandy bent to scoop the little dog up in her arms. Her eyes were bright and healthy, her coat soft and fluffy. She looked plump and well – a picture of health.

Mandy's throat was so full of happiness she couldn't speak.

'I thought you'd like to take her to Mrs Platt yourself,' Betty explained.

'Oh, I would.' Mandy, looked at her with shining eyes. Then she looked at her mother. 'Shall I ring her now, Mum? I've got time to go over before tea. I can groom Charley a bit later.'

'If you like, sweetheart.'

Mandy ran back inside. 'Jean, can you give me Mrs Platt's number?'

Jean thumbed through the card index and came up with Mrs Platt's telephone number.

'Thanks.' Mandy quickly dialled. After two rings she heard Mrs Platt's voice at the other end.

'Mrs Platt,' she said breathlessly. 'It's Mandy Hope.'

'Hello, Mandy.' Mrs Platt sounded pleased to hear her.

Mandy quickly explained about Antonia. She heard Mrs Platt draw in her breath.

'Oh, Mandy.' Mrs Platt's voice trembled a little. 'How lovely. Yes . . . please bring her over straight away.'

Mandy ran back outside. 'It's OK!' she cried. 'I can take her now. I won't be long, Mum.' She took the lead from Betty's hand. 'Thanks, Betty.'

Mandy felt really proud to be walking along with Antonia. She had helped to save the little dog's life and was taking her to a wonderful new home. It was a great feeling.

Antonia trotted meekly beside Mandy, as good as gold, all the way to Mrs Platt's bungalow. When they arrived, Mandy spied Mrs Platt watching eagerly from the window.

The door opened. Mrs Platt stood with a wide smile on her face.

'Come in, come in.' She wrung her hands in delight. Mandy felt her heart turn over as she handed Mrs Platt her new pet. Mrs Platt cradled the poodle's soft coat against her face. Then she held the dog away from her to get a better look.

'She's wonderful, Mandy! Thank you so much.' She hugged the dog to her again, then laughed as Antonia licked her face.

Mandy's throat ached. It was really great to see Mrs Platt so happy. 'Her name's Antonia,' she told her.

Antonia wagged her tail and licked Mrs Platt's nose.

'What a grand name! She's beautiful, Mandy.' Mrs Platt put Antonia down on the floor and gave Mandy a quick hug. 'I certainly won't be lonely any more,' she said, smiling. Then her smile broadened. She pointed. 'Well, bless me. Look at that!'

Antonia had jumped up on to Mrs Platt's fireside chair. 'Antonia!' Mandy chided.

'Well, who can blame her after all she's been through,' Mrs Platt said. 'Mind you, I don't think I'll fit very well into her basket!'

Mandy was still smiling as she said goodbye. Mrs Platt scooped Antonia off the chair and went with her to the door.

Mrs Platt kissed Mandy's cheek. 'Thank you again, Mandy. I'll never forget your kindness.' She and Antonia watched as Mandy went out of the gate. A little way down the road Mandy turned to wave. She didn't think she would ever forget the sight of Mrs Platt standing with Antonia tucked comfortably under her arm as if they had been friends for ever.

After tea, Mrs Hope drove Mandy and Charley up to Bleakfell Hall. Jess went along for the ride.

The new animal trainer greeted them at the back door. She was a young woman with short, red hair. She wore a pair of denim dungarees over a check shirt. A badge on the collar said 'Stop Animal Experiments'.

'Hi, I'm Sue.' She bent down. 'Hello, Charley, I'm so glad to meet you at last.' Charley wagged

her tail happily. Sue fondled Charley's neck and gave Jess a pat.

Mandy looked at her mum. She gave a sigh of relief. Charley would be OK now. She and Sue were already friends.

'Mrs Hope,' Sue said, 'one of the horses cut herself today. Would you take a look?'

'Yes, of course,' Mrs Hope said.

'Would you take Charley indoors for me, Mandy?' Sue asked.

'I'd love to.'

Mandy took Charley and Jess into the kitchen. She'd been dying to see Mr Baggins again. And the cats, of course – and everyone else.

Mr Baggins sat on his perch. The cats were asleep by the fire. Charley and Jess went straight into the pantry. When Mandy looked they were lying side by side on Charley's blanket. *I'm definitely not the only one who's going to miss Charley*, Mandy thought.

'*Right, everyone*,' said Mr Baggins. A noise like hands clapped together came from his throat.

Mandy couldn't help giggling. Mr Baggins sounded just like Hammond Curtis. She wondered what *he* thought about Mr Baggins's new saying.

'*In your places and two sugars,*' the parrot squawked.

Mandy ruffled the bright feathers. 'Been behaving yourself, Mr B?'

'No, he hasn't!' Ben Burton came through the door. Charley came out of the pantry to greet him. 'Charley! Great to see you, girl.' Charley licked his hand.

'I'm really going to miss Charley,' Mandy said.

Ben put his arm round her shoulders. 'She looks great, Mandy. You've all done a really good job. Hey, why not come up to see the filming tomorrow. Bring James if you like.'

'I'll ask Mum,' Mandy said, feeling more cheerful. 'But I'm sure it'll be OK.'

Mandy and Mrs Hope were driving back to Animal Ark when Mandy remembered she was going to ask about Jess.

'Mum . . .' She gazed at her mother thoughtfully. 'Is Jess . . . ?'

She noticed a twinkle in her mother's eye as she glanced at her.

'Is Jess what, Mandy?'

Mandy shifted in her seat. 'Is Jess by any chance . . . ?'

Mrs Hope laughed out loud. 'Come on, Mandy. Spit it out.'

'Is Jess . . . ?'

'Yes, Mandy,' Mrs Hope said, still laughing. 'Jess *is* going to have puppies!'

Ten

'I thought so!' Mandy shouted gleefully. 'Mum, why didn't you tell me?'

'We thought we'd keep it as a surprise. We might have known you'd spot she was getting more than just podgy.'

Mandy clasped her hands together. 'Mum, isn't it great? What's Auntie Mary going to say?'

Mrs Hope made a wry face. 'I don't know. I expect Tad is the father.'

Mandy laughed. 'I thought Jess was missing

him. I didn't know they were *such* good friends!' She turned round to look at the little terrier curled up on the back seat. 'Oh, Jess, you clever thing!' She felt she could burst with excitement. 'When, Mum . . . when is she having them?'

'Now calm down, Mandy,' Mrs Hope said, patting her daughter's knee. 'We're not quite sure . . . pretty soon though.'

'We must get things ready,' Mandy said. 'She'll need somewhere to have them. She likes the broom cupboard, I found her tearing up—'

Mandy's mother laughed again. 'Mandy, hold your horses. It won't be quite yet. Don't go turning out the cupboard just yet.'

'But she'll need somewhere,' Mandy insisted.

'We'll find her somewhere, don't worry,' Mrs Hope soothed.

Back at Animal Ark, Mandy skipped into the surgery with Jess. Mr Hope was just clearing up after the last patient.

'Dad, Mum's told me about Jess!'

Mr Hope smiled broadly. 'We thought you'd probably guess.'

'I did. I just had so much to think about I kept forgetting to ask. Oh, Dad, I'm so thrilled.' She picked Jess up gently and patted her stomach. Then she hugged the terrier close. Charley didn't need her now but soon there would be lots of other dogs to look after. Tiny, gorgeous Jack Russell puppies. She just couldn't wait!

Next morning, Mr Hope dropped them off at Bleakfell Hall for the day, complete with picnic lunch.

Mandy couldn't wait to tell Ben the good news about Jess.

'Congratulations, Jess!' Ben said when he heard. 'Sue said Charley's been moping around a bit. I expect she's been missing her.'

They found Sue grooming Charley in the kitchen. Charley looked great – a beautiful shining coat, moist nose. Mandy felt proud to have been the one to help rescue her.

Mr Baggins greeted them with his usual squawk.

'Better leave Jess in here,' said Sue, lifting Charley down from the grooming table. 'Charley will need all her concentration this morning.'

'Stay here, Jess,' Mandy began. But Jess was already curled up by the fire, fast asleep.

Mandy took a couple of pieces of orange from

a saucer on the table.

'Come on, Mr Baggins,' she called. 'Time for work.' Mr Baggins flew on to her shoulder.

They filed along the passageway and into the big hall.

'You'd better be good today, Mr Baggins,' Mandy whispered.

'*Yeah, yeah,*' said Mr Baggins.

In the big hall, Mandy placed the parrot gently on his perch. Everyone was ready.

'Right, over here with Charley, please.' Mr Curtis stepped forward.

'You take her over.' Sue handed the lead to Mandy.

'*Right . . . take your places,*' said a voice.

Everyone started to move into their positions.

'Did I say move?' Mr Curtis shouted. His face looked red with annoyance. 'Everyone stay where they are.'

'*Right . . . take your places.*' His voice came again.

The actors and crew looked at one another. Mandy burst out laughing. 'It's Mr Baggins,' she spluttered. Beside her, James put his hand over his mouth to control his laughter. All the crew were laughing too – even the man with the dagger sticking out of his chest.

'*Right . . . take your cup of tea,*' Mr Baggins squawked suddenly.

Even Mr Curtis was laughing by now. He wiped his eyes and waved his hand in the air. 'That's enough, thank you, Mr Baggins. *I'll* give the orders if you don't mind!' He pushed his cap to the back of his head. 'Never work with children or animals!' he said, grinning.

Then filming began in earnest. Before they knew it, it was almost lunch-time. After thirty-six takes, they had finally got the stabbing scene right.

'How would you like to be stabbed thirty-six times?' James whispered.

Mandy nudged him. 'Shh!'

Mr Baggins had been unusually quiet. He sat on his perch, a piece of orange skin in his claw. Once he tucked his head under his wing and went to sleep. No one seemed to notice. Except Antonia Kent. She kept a wary eye on Mr Baggins, whatever he did.

'Could you take Charley back to the kitchen please, young lady?' Mr Curtis sat on the top of a stepladder, looking down. 'Come back and watch the rest of the day's shoot if you like.'

'I'd love to,' breathed Mandy. 'Thanks.'

She quickly took Charley back to the kitchen. 'Stay,' she commanded, pushing her inside the door and closing it firmly. She didn't want to miss anything. Sue had already gone off to groom the horses.

It was another hour before Mr Curtis shouted, 'OK, everyone, take a break. We're outside this afternoon, don't forget.'

Everyone breathed a sigh of relief.

'Come on,' James said. 'I'm starving. Let's have our picnic!'

In the kitchen, the dogs were nowhere to be seen. The pantry door was slightly ajar.

'I bet the dogs are in there.' Mandy pushed open the pantry door. She peeped in. Charley was sitting in one corner. She pricked up her ears and looked at Mandy. She whined softly. It was as if she was trying to tell Mandy something – something very important.

Then there was another small sound. A whine and a series of tiny squeaks. Mandy opened the door a little more and went inside. She stopped suddenly. Her mouth fell open.

For there beside Jess, on Charley's blanket, were four squirming bundles. Tiny puppies, their eyes closed tight. Two black and white, two brown and white. So small they would fit into Mandy's palm. Jess was trying to lick them all at once. She glanced up at Mandy. 'Look,' she seemed to be saying. 'Aren't I clever?'

Mandy's eyes felt as if they were popping out of her head. 'James . . . here – quick!'

Jess – with four tiny puppies. It was just too good to be true!

James pulled a face. 'Wow! Aren't they . . . um – funny.'

'They're not *funny*,' Mandy said, feeling indignant. 'They're gorgeous.'

'They'll look a bit better when they're dry,' James muttered.

'Shh,' Mandy said. 'Jess will be insulted if she hears you.'

'They're lovely, Jess,' James said quickly. 'Wonderful.'

Soon all the film crew knew about the puppies in the pantry.

'We'd better leave her now,' Mandy said when they had all taken a peep. 'When Dad comes back we'll ask him what we should do.'

Just as she spoke, she heard her father's Land-rover pull up in the yard.

She ran outside. 'Dad! Dad, guess what?'

Mr Hope got out of the car. 'What now?'

Mandy pulled his arm to drag him inside. 'Jess's had her puppies. In the pantry!'

'The pantry! Well, trust Jess. She always did like her food.'

Mr Hope came in to examine the pups. 'They're all fine,' he said. 'We don't want to upset Jess, so we'll leave them here for tonight, if that's OK?' he said to Sue. 'We'll collect them first thing tomorrow.'

Suddenly Jess wagged her tail furiously. There, peeping from behind Mr Hope's legs, was Charley. Jess whined and Charley pushed through into the pantry.

'I think Charley better stay out,' Mr Hope began.

Mandy touched his arm. 'No, Dad,' she whispered. 'Look!'

Charley was licking one of Jess's puppies.

Mandy stood watching, her hands on her hips.
'She's going to be their auntie,' she said.

Everyone laughed. Mr Hope gave his daughter
a hug. 'Fancy having a film star for an auntie,' he
said, a broad grin spreading across his face.

'We'll come back first thing,' Mr Hope reassured
Mandy as they drove back to Animal Ark. 'Jess is
in good hands for tonight.'

'In good paws you mean,' James piped up from
the back seat.

The next day, the film crew were packing up
when they arrived to collect Jess. The rest of the

movie would be made at the studio.

'I shall really miss you all,' Mandy said to Ben, giving him a hug.

'If you change your mind about being a vet, Mandy,' Hammond Curtis came down the stairs, a suitcase in his hand, 'just give me a ring. I'll find you a job as an animal trainer.'

'Thanks, Mr Curtis,' Mandy said, shaking his hand. 'But I don't think I will.'

Sue walked in with Mr Baggins in a cage. Charley followed at her heels. Mandy poked her finger through the bars of Mr Baggins's cage. 'Now, you behave yourself, Mr Baggins.'

'*Two cups of sugar*,' Mr Baggins said, looking annoyed at being shut in.

Mandy bent to hug Charley, sad at having to say goodbye. ''Bye, Charley, I'll watch for you on TV.'

Jess was safely tucked in the back of the Land-rover with her pups. Mandy squared her shoulders as she watched Charley clamber into the Animal Stars van. Jess and her little family needed her now. Her job with Charley was over.

'Come on then, Dad,' she said. 'Let's get Jess and her babies home.'

Mandy turned to take one final look at Bleakfell Hall as they drove through the wrought iron gates and headed for home.

Ahead, the winding road led down to the village. Mandy felt full of anticipation. Four puppies to care for until Aunt Mary came home from Australia! And Jess, of course. What fun they were going to have.

She wound down the window and took a deep breath of sharp, clear air. She could see the village now, nestling peacefully among great stretches of moorland. The familiar church spire rose comfortingly from the bundle of houses and shops. She would feel really special, walking Jess and her four puppies across the village green for all to see. And when it was time for them to go back home Mandy knew there would be plenty of other animals needing her care. She grinned to herself. *Life*, she thought happily, *is absolutely great!*

Read more about Animal Ark in
Kittens in Trouble

One

'Mandy, you're very keen on school all of a sudden,' Mr Hope said. He watched her stuff old newspapers into her schoolbag. She flung on her school jacket, flicked a brush through her dark blonde hair and snatched a mouthful of toast. 'It's only ten to eight. Are you sure you're OK?'

'Very funny!' Mandy said. 'Of course I'm OK. It's just a special day, that's all.' She'd fed her rabbits and done her morning chores at Animal Ark. Simon, the nurse, had come in to take over care of the animals and do temperatures and medicines. Now she was free to go.

'School trip?' Mr Hope took a guess as Mandy unlocked her bicycle padlock and put on her crash-helmet. He got no reply. 'New boyfriend?'

'Ha, ha!' Mandy said. 'No time now, Dad. I'll tell you later.' She set off up the front drive, her long legs pedalling like mad. She waved at her mother.

'What's the rush?' Mrs Hope wound down her car window.

But Mandy had already sped by, under the wooden sign, 'Animal Ark, Veterinary Surgeon'. She took one look back at the old stone cottage with its modern vets' extension to the rear, then she pedalled hard again. Her heavy schoolbag dragged across her shoulder.

'She's up to something,' Mandy heard Mrs Hope say. 'She's got that determined look on her face.'

Mandy knew they wouldn't have a clue what she wanted with the old newspapers. But she ignored them and charged up the lane towards Welford village. She'd keep her mystery until evening, after Mrs Hope came back from her round of visits to the sick cats, dogs, goats and hamsters that made up the busy practice of Animal Ark.

She gave her mum and dad one last wave
before she turned out on to the road. 'See you
later!' she yelled.

'This is it! This is the big day!' Mandy greeted
her friend, James Hunter. As usual, his straight
brown hair flopped on to his forehead, and his
glasses sat halfway down his nose.

'Hi,' he said. 'Do you realise I've dragged
myself out of bed half an hour early to meet up
with you outside this rotten post office!' He
was breathless from pedalling. 'My dad nearly
dropped dead with shock!'

'Come on!' Mandy said, ignoring his protests,
'Let's go and see!'

Mandy and James cycled out of Welford
on the two mile stretch into Walton. Past all
the sleepy cottages and wide awake farms with
their collie dogs at the gate, she never once
stopped chattering.

'It's going to be today, I know it!' She had a
feeling about these things. James nodded and
panted to keep up. 'I'm so excited, I can hardly
wait!' The ground sped by under their wheels.
'She's been looking for a warm dry place, and

that's always a sign! Anyway, she refused her food yesterday.' James nodded again in agreement. 'I did see her in the caretaker's porch yesterday after school, behind the stack of logs. She's a very clever cat!'

They pedalled down the final hill. Mandy's short hair blew back in the wind. The new bungalows of Walton greeted them, spick and span. Walton Moor School lay behind these new houses; another new building which backed on to open countryside. Mandy and James rode through the gateway into the deserted playground.

Mr Williams, the caretaker, strode through the grounds, setting out parking cones for the dustbin lorry. It was Thursday, bin day. 'Morning!' Mandy called, with James running to catch up. But Mr Williams was a man of few words. He ignored her greeting.

'Shh, now!' Mandy warned James. They'd left their bikes locked up in the shed, and came up behind the caretaker's house. 'We don't want to disturb her.' Carefully they peered over the beech hedge, neatly trimmed by Mr Williams. They scanned his pink rose bushes and the porch at the back of his house.

'Mandy,' James dared to whisper, 'does Mr Williams know about this?' He was cleaning his glasses on his school jumper. 'I mean, what will he say if he finds us snooping about on his porch?'

'He won't mind,' Mandy whispered back. How could anyone mind about animals? 'Mrs Williams sometimes puts out food. I expect that's why Walton has chosen their porch to have her babies in!' Mandy's face shone with excitement.

'Walton?' James didn't realise the cat had a name. It was small, black and white and rather ordinary. As far as he knew, it was a stray. But then Mandy had kept details about the cat pretty much to herself up till now.

'I named her after the school,' Mandy said. 'According to Mrs Williams, she just turned up on the main doorstep one night, dumped inside a plastic bag, with tiny airholes to breathe through. Can you believe it? People can be so cruel!'

Mandy could feel the prick of tears in her eyes even now. 'She was only a young cat and someone just dumped her!' She sniffed and tried to pull herself together. 'She would've died if I hadn't come along early next morning and gone to the staffroom for some milk for her. She was really neglected. I had to feed her up.' She squared her shoulders. 'Anyway, that was six weeks ago. She's the school cat now, only a sort of half stray. So it's up to us to look after her!'

With that, Mandy eased open the back gate into the Williams's garden. 'Walton! Walton!' she coaxed, bending low and looking under the stilted porch into the dark space there. James peered up on to the porch itself, behind the stack of logs. No cat.

'Walton!' Mandy called, a bit more loudly.

A black and white shape trotted across the long shadows of the lawn, and over the flower-bed; a round, heavy shape, nearly as wide as she was long, with a low belly. James spotted her first. 'Mandy, look!' he said.

Mandy breathed a sigh. They'd got here in time. 'Hello, Walton,' she said. 'Here's a nice, comfy place for you to give birth to your lovely kittens, see!' She climbed the porch steps. The cat followed. Mandy delved into her bag and drew out the old newspapers. She showed them to Walton and let her sniff them. 'See, nice and warm and dry!'

Animal Ark™

**For more information about
Animal Ark and for the latest news
on the books and how you can
get involved, visit the website:**

www.animalark.co.uk

Hodder
Children's
Books

A division of Hachette Children's Books